CALLS MAY
FOR TRA
MONITORIN

by

KATHARINA VOLCKMER

Should we really ever bring our whole selves to work?

In a London call centre, Jimmie helps holiday makers with myriad problems, but he is hardly a model employee. He doesn't simply provide customer service to his clients and advice to his colleagues, he gets involved in their fantasies and frustrations, and now he's about to be hauled up in front of the boss.

From perfecting his roles as an undertaker and as a clown to performing duties above and beyond his employment contract, he debates the importance of the optimum shade for lipstick and bathroom walls, the pros and cons of nudist versus textile, as well as the psychological impacts of an Italian mother and an emotional support animal.

This is the second, ribald, scatological novel from the brilliant author of *The Appointment*. Jimmie's sly, sharp, melancholy insights into the indignities of a world which aims to eliminate the human will make you laugh, weep and never look the same way at an electric carving knife again.

© Robin Christian

KATHARINA VOLCKMER was born in Germany in 1987. She now lives in London, where she works for a literary agency. Her first novel, *The Appointment*, has been translated into over fifteen languages and has been adapted for the stage and radio in several countries.

Praise for *Calls May Be Recorded for Training and Monitoring Purposes*

'This book is filled with brilliant dialogue, unexpected turns, some very dirty talk with sudden bursts of hilarity, and then fierce sadness. It exudes dark energy. It is highly original. It gives pleasure on every page.' **Colm Tóibín, author of *Brooklyn* and *Long Island***

'Raucous, incisive and wholly original, the world of Volckmer's novel lays bare modern life's gross indignations, mordant desires and naked ambitions with wit and clarity.'

Eley Williams, author of *Moderate to Poor, Occasionally Good*

'This book reminds us of why we love Volckmer. She is a true iconoclast. Her work is a hand grenade thrown against the falsities of good taste.' **Carlos Fonseca, author of *Austral***

'The writing is agile . . . the sub-text contains more social criticism than at first meets the eye. It's a truculent novel which takes full responsibility for itself.' ***Vogue France***

'Iconoclastic, derisive and scatological. It could have been puerile if it were not written so intelligently, with such perfection.' ***Echo***

'Katharina Volckmer has created an unforgettable, ultra-contemporary personality.' ***Lire***

'The author plunges her pen, as funny as it is fierce, into a perfect microcosm, containing all the vices of our sad modern world. It leaves behind stains and a nasty smell, but it bubbles with great spirit.' ***Focus Vif***

'The reader frequently giggles at this satire whose irreverence and sweet madness reminds us of Shalom Auslander.' ***Libération***

'A funny, acerbic, and filter-free portrait of the world of work and contemporary vacuities.' ***Page***

Praise for *The Appointment*

A *TLS* Book of the Year 2020

'Surprising, inventive, disturbing and beautiful – *The Appointment* is an overdue, radical intervention.'

Chris Kraus, author of *I Love Dick*

'Katharina Volckmer is a risk-taker of the first degree. Her monologue is of hypnotic, lyrical invention and wit, coruscating self-loathing, profound pessimism and fragile hope. As dark and brilliant as *The Naked Lunch*. *The Appointment* is also mesmerisingly beautiful.'

Ian McEwan, author of *The Cockroach*

'[A] transgressive, darkly funny novel.'

New Yorker

'Katharina Volckmer's debut, *The Appointment*, is the most audacious novel I have read in years… [It] is horribly funny and shockingly good; if the best writing takes a risk, this is Russian roulette.'

Frances Wilson, *TLS*

'Audacious… hilariously funny. The prose is immaculate, she captures you, buttonholes you from the very first page… It is better than it has any right to be for a first book.'

Backlisted

'At once sexy, hilarious, and subversive, the book is also acutely sad. Desire, in this novel, takes many forms: the desire to be heard, the desire to be otherwise, the desire for a different past and a different future.'

Paris Review

'*The Appointment* is serious and challenging. Volckmer movingly explores the complexities not only of [the narrator's] gender identity but also of all those living against the grain, looking out from the margins at those whose existences are "immediately understandable for everyone".'

Alexander Leissle, *TLS*

'Powerfully addresses genocide, gender identity, and transphobia.'

Lily Hart Meyersohn, *Los Angeles Review of Books*

CALLS MAY BE RECORDED FOR TRAINING AND MONITORING PURPOSES

CALLS MAY BE RECORDED FOR TRAINING AND MONITORING PURPOSES

KATHARINA VOLCKMER

THE
INDIGO
PRESS

THE INDIGO PRESS
50 Albemarle Street
London W1S 4BD
www.theindigopress.com

The Indigo Press Publishing Limited Reg. No. 10995574
Registered Office: Wellesley House, Duke of Wellington Avenue
Royal Arsenal, London SE18 6SS

First published in Great Britain in 2025 by The Indigo Press

First published in French in 2024 by Éditions Grasset & Fasquelle as *Wonderfuck* by Katharina Volckmer

A CIP catalogue record for this book is available from the British Library

ISBN: 978-1-911648-89-5
eBook ISBN: 978-1-911648-90-1

Cover design © JF Paga
Cover image © Ferrantraite | Getty images
Art direction by House of Thought
Typeset by Tetragon, London
Printed and bound in Great Britain by TJ Books, Padstow

EU GPSR Authorised Representative
LOGOS EUROPE, 9 rue Nicolas Poussin, 17000, LA ROCHELLE, France
E-mail: Contact@logoseurope.eu

1 3 5 7 9 8 6 4 2

For Maurizio. With love.

In memory of Adeline Stuart-Watt

Instead of committing suicide, people go to work.

THOMAS BERNHARD, *Correction*

If you are going to shit yourself, it's most likely to happen on your own doorstep. Just as your cat, as you carry it home from the vet, will suddenly grow violent inside its carrier – sensing its imminent freedom and the smells of a territory it fought many dirty battles over – so too will your bowels surrender the moment you can picture the comfort of a familiar toilet seat. The soft feel of an appliance built for our most private needs. The delicious space that only a locked door can offer. The stillness that Jimmie often felt so exposed without. And like the cat that no longer feels bound to behave itself away from the constraints of an unfamiliar world, your body will also give in, knowing that on the other side of the door there is no one you care enough about to stop you from that most vile of all hygiene violations. That loss of self-control that would render anyone painfully unfuckable. An act of submission that only arouses the disturbed, the wealthy men that feed sex workers curries so they shit more quickly. But even those men might struggle to get off on shitty pants, because nobody gets off on failure.

Jimmie looked at the expensive dogs and babies on the bus he was taking into work, wondering whether they were all fitted with special nappies that would immediately alert their owners in the event of a disgrace. Shielding them from our primordial fear of excrement and the diseases it carries, the fear we feel for our bodies. The instinct that tells us that this is far worse than wetting your bed, that no childhood trauma will ever be endearing enough to justify those brown stains. Because those stains are for old and damaged people in care homes, or the people Jimmie would sometimes see on this bus route. Bodies that had lost the fight with their own fluids, one step away from ultimate misery. Those stains are the actual colour of death. Fading bodily functions, briefly hidden beneath flowers and grief.

If it's done properly – and it's not some misguided strangulation involving a heated towel rail – you will shit yourself if you are hung. (Or hang yourself, depending on your circumstances.) Revealing the truth behind that last dropping sound, only briefly disguised by the snapping of a neck. It was one of his mother's better stories: a neighbour back home who had failed to end her life that way. Too lazy to climb up on a chair and use a hook, she had tried to get away with sinking to the bathroom floor, her dog's old leash around her neck, tied to the towel rail. Jimmie sensed the woman's humiliation. He knew that his own body would also have been too clumsy to perform this seemingly impossible act of strangulation. His weight would rip the rail from the wall before any loss of consciousness could set him free, the inevitable cracks revealing the rot in the house's foundations. His mother was right. There was nothing delicate about such final moments, just as there was nothing delicate about his current predicament, for there is no beauty in a heart that has lost its way. Like a nocturnal animal dragged from its cave and left at the mercy of the forces that operate in daylight, Jimmie had forgotten how to move with grace.

From what he remembered, he hadn't felt like dying that day, or at least not to the extent that he'd considered all the possible options and their impact on the remains of his dignity. That had been before he'd found himself taking this bus to work in the mornings, before the dogs and babies with rich parents had made him feel poor. Before he knew that his desires had no respect for his feelings and that seat belts on aeroplanes are not there to keep us safe but to make it easier to identify our bodies in case of a disaster.

That day, as he tried to put his keys in the lock, forever forgetting which one to use for the front door, he had felt his muscles go soft. It was as if his body had decided to take over the narrative, to tell the story his mind would never find the right words for. To react before he could understand what had really happened at the funeral parlour. Jimmie had never felt much in control and, as if to confirm this, he now felt the wrong kind of warmth between his cheeks. It was confirmation that life is not just a cruel joke, because at least a cruel joke would give you something to laugh about.

But there was nothing to laugh about when he felt his own shit running down the inside of his leg, about to break free and land on his mother's doormat, when he worried that he'd lose his wallet and the dead man's hair he'd put in there to keep it safe. It was before Elin could tell him that in the absence of trousers a bra strap offers better storage than a dress sleeve. That all elastics are treacherous creatures and pockets are an essential part of the female revolution. There was also nothing to cry about, because those were not the sensations of a real problem – a leg that was about to look like he was wearing a dishevelled Nazi uniform beneath his mother's old, oversized summer dress, wondering which bits of his unreasonable diet had found their way to freedom once more.

All of this was in the past now, as far away as his youth or the last time he had seen his mother smile. Unreachable, like the notion of pleasure when you're on your way to work. As he had done for many days now, Jimmie was getting ready to become the person his colleagues expected to see, and as he stared at the other people on the bus, all trying to exist in a space they'd rather not share, trying to avoid the memories their bodies had produced, he finally understood that it was simply nothing. A void. An impenetrable darkness in which all he could make out were his body's angry reactions to his pathetic existence. Nothing but the silence of his own ambitions.

A day.

'Thank you for waiting. My name is Jimmie. How can I help you today?'

'You know that thing about sharks, how they can smell a drop of blood from miles away? I have a skin condition that makes me scratch quite a bit. Can you guarantee that I will be safe in the waters outside Mykonos?'

'You do realize that Mykonos is in Greece, sir?'

'Are you trying to tell me that there are no sharks in the Mediterranean?'

The lipstick had begun to crumble at the corners of Jimmie's mouth. The cheap red lipstick that he wanted his lover to see. He had stolen it from one of the many little boxes in his mother's bedroom the night before, when he'd come home from work to find her asleep. His mother, the Signora. The most widowed widow of them all. The Italian lady with the unpronounceable surname: Bevilacqua. Asleep for most of her life, afraid of the colours outside her bedroom, forever in love with her own sadness – a life hidden beneath dust and unwanted bits of sympathy. A tragedy with only her son as an audience. A drama wasted on a new country that would never be more than her unfinished dream.

'What about the sharks then?'

'Do you reckon your blood has the same colour as my lipstick?'

'Excuse me?'

'I'm just trying to picture it. You and your broken skin, the deep blue sea and the villain with the scary teeth. Have you been thinking of a great white shark?'

'Are you out of your mind?'

'I'm just a very visual person, and since we've been trained to take our customers' concerns seriously, I want to see what you're seeing. Where exactly do you tend to scratch? Don't you think it's likely that's where the shark will attack first?'

'Fucking freak.'

The voice gone, Jimmie imagined a cloud of blood pouring forth from a severed middle-aged limb with bits of flesh and a pair of those fancy multicoloured swimming trunks floating around. Underwater cries muffled by the violence of the sea. He suddenly envied the shark its freedom to fulfil its urges, and he decided to follow the animal's example and mute his telephone even though the first hour of his shift wasn't up. Even though the rules of the call centre didn't allow him to get up to stare at himself in the mirror for a minute, or to cry into his unbuttoned trousers on one of those unhinged toiled seats. But Jimmie didn't care, because he wanted today to be a different day. A soft day. Like a subtle shade of pink. A day without hurt.

He tried to quickly get past the endless rows of desk pods belonging to the other teams on his floor. Clusters of little round space stations representing the various products people could call for from a comfortable distance, like their veg boxes, dog food, mattresses and toilet paper. Or in Jimmie's case: their holidays. The affiliation of each cluster was made visible by a cheap cardboard sign with a company name and logo floating above the employees. Held by invisible strings, these loomed overhead like a constant menace, part of an apparatus that was ready to come crashing down on those caught being unproductive or unhelpful. Team members were identifiable by their one item of corporate identity, the different hoodies they had to wear, with the exception of the team leaders and managers, who were allowed to enjoy the comforts of civilian life while everyone else looked and felt like a Teletubby. The hoodies reminded Jimmie of sheep whose fleece was tagged by their owners in bright colours. As he walked past his colleagues now, he recognized some faces. But most of them were new and unknown, even though he had already spent almost a year working at Vanilla Travels Ltd.

At least he wasn't working on the outbound floor below, where he'd have to offer his last resources and make cold calls, or in one of the even more miserable call centres abroad. At least his customers needed him, even if it was only a fleeting dependence, so he wasn't constantly getting insulted and stepped on like a creature that had been labelled a pest. And yet he was still part of a never-ending abundance, a set of bones that had no right to ask for dignity. The voice of a person who was invisible outside these walls. As much as he sometimes liked the idea of not having this body, he knew that the time might have come to be brave and face a world where his fat curves would be a reality once again.

As he locked the toilet door behind him, Jimmie remembered that he had agreed to spend his long break today with Elin, his Swedish friend from the booking team who dreamed of opening an outdoor nursery in a forest. Elin always looked like she had a cat's arse on her face, her lips tight, as if she had tried to pleasure a bag of lemons. Leaving aside the lack of any genuine wildlife in London, Jimmie could never imagine leaving children in her care. They would probably return as little forest weirdos with premature beards covering their faces, sinister garden gnomes who refused to sing and dance. Maybe it was a special Swedish survival technique: no need to be cheerful when it was just you and those endless woods filled with the good life and elks. Or moose? Jimmie had no idea what the difference was. Elin had shown him a picture once, and those big bodies on skinny legs had reminded him of his grandmother and how she had pushed her heavy torso through life like a shopping trolley. It must have been her genes that had made him look like this.

With his face trying to reach the space between his legs, Jimmie managed to avoid looking at the faded orange meant to lend a human touch to the toilet cubicle with its fake surfaces. This boudoir of the modern office worker. Unlike grey, orange was so confident in its ugliness. It had always made him slightly jealous, as though it were possible to be so bold about your imperfections. He regretted what this place had witnessed. How these thin walls had celebrated his defeat. With his underwear still fresh, he managed to catch a whiff of his own smells, his home and laundry detergent – a reminder that he was still alive – while he tried to think back to his last conversation with Elin, earlier that week. She had been eating vegetarian Pot Noodles, which always made him feel sick. He was sure that if he hadn't been forced to leave Italy he would never have been exposed to such culinary abuse. Even now, as he tried to bury his head in his own lap, his belly preventing him from producing an elegant shape, he could see Elin shoving those slippery worms into her tiny cat-arse mouth smothered in neon lipstick.

'Who are you trying to fuck?'

'What?'

'Your lipstick. Do you have plans? Or are you worried that our customers can see you through the phone and will only book a holiday if there's some visual stimulation?' Jimmie pretended to be choking on a dick until she blushed.

'Piss off, Jimmie. But if you must know – yes, I'm going on a date.'

'The guy from the veg box team?'

Looking at her he often wondered whether fillers, like those Helena had injected so successfully into her own face, might help alleviate the problem of her uninviting lips, but figured that when it came to it even a real cat's back door would probably be more appealing.

'I went on one date with him, Jimmie.'

'I imagine it was hard to climax to the ecological benefits of root vegetables.'

'Very funny.'

'Is it someone from the toilet paper team this time? Maybe you'll learn how to squirt on peach-scented two-ply softness.'

'No, and before you start fantasizing about the people from the dog food team, it's actually Simon. We are going for a drink after our shift.'

'Our supervisor? The angry ginger boy?'

'Shut up. And you had better not tell Daniel about it.'

'Please don't tell me he's doing another one of those terrible granola bar ads!'

'Don't pretend you don't know.'

Gossip usually flowed through Jimmie's veins like bubbles of comfort and joy, but this time, as Elin's words started to reveal their true meaning, his heart refused to steady its course.

'You mean they've made Daniel team leader now that Stuart has left?'

'Correct. As of this Friday, your darling won't have to wear a yellow hoodie any more.'

All of a sudden, Jimmie felt inferior even to Elin's tiny cat-arse mouth, killing any erotic potential he had ever found in his own full lips. Why hadn't Daniel told him about this? Why had he made him sit in this pathetic kitchen with Elin, looking like two lost losers whose only chance in life was to fuck the people in charge? It was as if things with Daniel were now something to be ashamed of, like his pride had been touched in the wrong place. And then he pictured Elin's neon lipstick on Simon's cock, and all the colours were out of sync. When had she learned to play with all that life beneath her skin? How had she found the confidence to give pleasure, when he felt trapped in discomfort and longing?

Now, as he listened to the sweet radio station that filled all areas outside the call centre floor like an American torture cell, Jimmie felt his body reacting to this absence of silence. He felt his tissues losing resistance as he tried to understand how nerves could be so treacherous as to pass on the information he could so easily have lived without. How they were ready to dance when he tried to contain himself. How they would tell on him when he stepped on a wasp in his mother's garden as a child, allowing pain to travel all the way up to his mind and finally his eyes. If pain was nothing but the result of successful communication somewhere in his brain, why couldn't the unseen just stay in the dark? Why wasn't it enough to bleed from the wounds that fingers could heal? Even now, when he was supposed to be at his desk in the corner, dealing with his daily emails and phone calls – the utterings of people at odds with their own hedonism, holidays made unenjoyable by their own expectations – why did life suddenly feel like he had once again stepped into the rage of a dying creature?

'Jimmie. Are you in there? It's Simon.'

Of course it was him. Naturally hostile towards the illicit, Simon was raiding their last bit of privacy, suspecting pleasure where he only wanted to see effort. He was always ready to get down on his knees to count the number of legs in a cubicle, and Jimmie hated the guilt he felt because of it. Like his body was taking up too much space, like Simon had a right to inspect his desires. And he didn't even have any cold water to cool his eyes. Why didn't these fucking cubicles come with a sink, a mirror and a bit of the luxury he read about in hotel descriptions all day?

'I'm sorry. I'll be out in a minute.'

'You do know that you have to check with me first before going on a break, right? It's a busy floor today and we cannot have people going on breaks together.'

Impossible not to hear the suspicions, not to feel yourself shrinking inside.

'Are you sure you're okay, Jimmie? Do you need help?'

'I'm all right. Just having a slow start, you know?'

Simon surely didn't: he had been born with that disgusting type of energy that enabled him to jump out of bed in the morning and iron his shirts. He never felt the need to question his erections or lock himself into a cheap orange toilet because he couldn't face the prospect of another day on this earth. Jimmie couldn't believe that Elin had agreed to go on a second date with him tonight.

'I'm hardly going to slash my wrists in here. And I'm not having a party either – I have a little more taste than that.' He might as well ask to be buried by Mr John Nobes, his former employer and owner of a funeral parlour, purveyor of the ugliest coffins in town.

'Can you please open the door, Jimmie? Otherwise I will have to escalate this incident.'

Perhaps he could have taken over the business and become a funeral master. He could have made peace with things and then guaranteed that people and their pets were dealt with for good. He could have offered cremations only, just to be sure.

'Jimmie! You missed the meeting this morning, and I really need to talk to you during your break today.'

'And if I have plans?'

'Then I'm afraid you will have to cancel them. This is rather urgent. I'm sure you know what it's about.'

Jimmie didn't bother checking his looks on his phone camera, because he knew that he didn't have any today and he wasn't ready for what the light in this toilet would reveal.

Simon was leaning against the sink opposite the cubicle. In another version of Jimmie's life he might have stopped there and looked into Simon's inquisitive blue eyes. It could have been flirtation or even a kiss, a moment of meaning and intimacy. A first step towards something tender, or even something rough. The beginning of something warm. But instead, he remembered that he was wearing his mother's lipstick and that everything around them smelled of piss and other bodily functions, and all he could do was walk past Simon, who didn't even try to hide his surprise at Jimmie's new colours. His eyes on the floor, Jimmie tried to forget that this had been an act of transgression, that he was almost thirty and his left hand was shaking because of an unauthorized toilet break.

Doing the late shift meant that Jimmie mostly missed out on the early team meetings during which Simon dissected one or two calls that had been recorded for those famous training and monitoring purposes. His colleagues were forced to witness each other's performances being taken apart like dead frogs. To watch the remains of their pride grow cold and unappealing in the hands of a man with a sharp blade. Among all the recorded calls, Simon always managed to find the one instance where their overall high-quality track record hadn't been maintained, where a call centre agent had failed to respond appropriately or make their customer feel at ease. Like a hand-job with the wrong amount of lube. Or a pig's nipple on a piece of bacon suddenly bringing down the illusions of fast food.

Bodies get in the way.

Simon was their sinister master, punishing them for their failings by shaming them in public – all proof of the fact that he had to be in regular contact with the mystery caller, that cursed tool of quality control they all lived in fear of. The spectre with a million different voices that they could hear behind each disharmony, there to lead them astray like children in a forest. Jimmie often pictured them like a witch in a house made of temptations, longing to turn their tired bodies into a feast. Simon liked to remind his team that they needed to bend over further and make others happy and never forget that they were not allowed to use the word 'compensation'. They were sentient beings, and this was about their soft skills. Everything Jimmie and his colleagues did was a gesture of goodwill, and customers could tell if their concerns weren't being taken seriously.

Soft skills. Whenever Simon used those words, Jimmie could feel his own soft parts becoming ticklish. He hated public exposure, but sometimes he liked to get off on Simon's anger, imagining other possible punishments they might experience together. Much as he suspected that some of the calls Simon enjoyed playing with during those meetings were his own, Jimmie also knew that as long as he was willing to do the late shift, they were unlikely to fire him. He knew how difficult it was to find someone who would work Friday and Saturday nights, someone who, instead of a life, had a mother and a cat. Someone like Jimmie.

Simon following him into the toilet to ask for a formal chat meant that this wasn't about one of Jimmie's usual calls, his recurring inability to adhere to company standards. It was proof that word of his latest adventure had travelled round the office like a willing boy, that the information had finally reached Simon's firm little ears and he now knew what Jimmie had done in the toilet last Friday.

Doing the late shift also meant that Jimmie was the last one to arrive and choose his seat, therefore having to make do with one of the more depleted headsets. Invariably, he had to sit next to Wolf, the weird German with the missing toes – a rumour Wolf had never confirmed nor disputed. Depending on who you listened to, it had either been a hiking accident or an unfortunate encounter with a piece of German engineering. Or a defect at birth. Every time he looked at Wolf's hiking boots, Jimmie was sure it was true; he could even picture the little mummified stumps, soft like the remains of an embalmed pope, and he struggled to think of the hills and other obstacles that required this kind of footwear in London. But perhaps some Germans were born with hiking boots? At least Wolf didn't wear sandals. Jimmie shuddered as he sat back down, hearing Wolf operate in his unfuckable mother tongue, wondering whether Germans really shouted *ja* when they tried to express affection. He also remembered how the pope washes strangers' feet and blames this weird fetish on a need to demonstrate modesty and devotion. But before he could think of touching Wolf's little stumps in an attempt to purify his soul, Jimmie's phone rang. He put on the headset used by so many others before him; the microphone was limp and greasy. It was like seeing someone coming out of the toilet you were about to use only to then find the warmth of their arse on your seat. The feeling that nothing is ever truly yours.

'Thank you for waiting. My name is Jimmie. How can I help you today?'

'I wonder if you *can* help me, Jimmie.'

'I can certainly try.'

'I'm calling about that offer you currently have on your website, the Romantic Spa Break outside Bath. What I want to know is how I can book this offer for a single person, because your website doesn't seem to give me the option?'

'You want to go on the Romantic Spa Break by yourself, madam?'

Jimmie tried to picture the caller, but instead of all the usual cat lady clichés he could only think of his mother. The born widow trying to check into the Heartbreak Hotel. He knew that he must have had a father once, but all that remained of him was the idea that there must have been a time when his mother was different.

'I don't care about all that romance stuff, I just want a spa break.'

'Let me quickly check if any of our other spa breaks have that option and I can put you through to one of my colleagues in the booking department. I'm only here to deal with complaints.'

'I don't think you understand. I want this particular spa break, but for myself.'

He pictured the woman entering the room. Some cheap rose petals strewn across the bed, the word LOVE written on every wall, its letters dripping down in fluids of never-ending lust. It was hard to fuck yourself out of that predicament.

'You could always book the offer on our website and let them know you're coming on your own.'

'And pay for two?'

'I'm afraid that's all I can think of right now.'

Jimmie found some happiness in the knowledge that most of the couples around him were too tired to touch each other and had looked at their partners for so long that they booked romantic weekends away to get over the shame of their unfulfillable desires. To pretend that they were all eating, fucking and shitting in unbreakable rows of happiness.

This woman was a true rebel, a hero with a whole wardrobe full of toys and dildos.

'Do you wear a cape on those occasions?'

'A cape?'

'Sorry. I got carried away.'

A super-dildo cape with pictures of only the most beautiful toys on it.

'Are you discriminating against single women then?'

'The same policy applies to men.'

'You know exactly what I mean.'

'Listen, I'll ring them up and see what I can do and then I'll call you back. How does that sound?'

'Make sure you don't forget. I believe the offer will only be on for another day or so, and I really need a break.'

'I won't. Trust me.'

Jimmie liked the idea of himself in a super-dildo cape, flying away into the night sky and not giving a fuck any more. Why would he even go for someone who fancied Elin's pink lips? Simon was the first Brit he'd ever had the hots for, and Jimmie still didn't understand why he was now following his mother's desire for these unhealthy-looking people. They were the ones who had turned polenta into a cake and put chicken on a pizza, and Simon wasn't even that attractive. With his freckled skin and that unrefined academic haircut, he almost gave Jimmie erections against his will.

'You know there is a list, right?' Wolf had taken off his headset and arranged it neatly on his desk. Jimmie was sure that he used wet wipes to clean his arse.

'A list?'

'Yes. A list with all the hotels offering single accommodation at a discounted rate.'

'Sorry. I didn't know.'

'It should have been mentioned during your training sessions, but I'm not surprised that it wasn't, given that Helena was your buddy. She was probably busy thinking about her musical theatre ambitions. I had a look while you were on the phone and this particular hotel doesn't offer any special rates, so I'm afraid she will have to pay the full price. It's a shame we're not offering any other options.'

'I guess you're a little too old to become a professional fuckboy.'

'That's not what I meant, Jimmie!'

'But then I'm sure you could get into it and bring some joy into some of these solitary lives.' Jimmie pushed his tongue through the *v* of his fingers, briefly feeling the strange sensation of his painted lips. He could tell that Wolf was looking at them, thinking he was being even weirder than usual.

'You should really try to avoid this kind of obscenity in the workplace, Jimmie. Some people might take offence, and you know what the rules are.'

Jimmie knew that they had a zero tolerance policy for all human urges and that according to their official handbook it was best to not have a body at all, to simply exist as an immaterial being that worked hard and didn't suffer from any kind of pain or longing. Not for the first time, he wondered why he didn't walk out of this infernal place and never come back. Trust that his body would write its own story outside the rules of this office – little moments of struggle that would one day be memories of love.

He decided to ring the hotel anyway next time Wolf was on one of his arse-wipe breaks. He wanted the dildo-cape lady to crush those fake rose petals with her self-made pleasure, and not to wait for someone like Wolf to get an erection once a year.

Jimmie bent down a bit so that Wolf couldn't see him across the little grey wall that was meant to separate their workspaces, an illusion of self-containment on their telephone pod island. He never understood why they were there or – since they were there – why they were never cleaned. Was that the point, to separate people by reminding them of all the traces their bodies left behind? All the particles of shit, sweat, dust and saliva that had slowly started to build on these surfaces. Something that looked like grease but had so much more to offer, that had set and changed colour over the years. That felt like a summary of his life written in a language he couldn't read but still understood. A reminder of everything that had gone wrong, how his lost dreams and intentions had solidified and become the face he saw every morning. A face that had more and more chins growing around it and no longer held enough beauty to encourage any genuine feeling in another. A face that would never be in a relationship, or that anyone would introduce to their parents, because his weren't the features of a good wife with purposeful hips. These stains that he could sense on all the surfaces around him were like the chewing gum marks on the pavement outside the office. The remains of our ability to recreate, to be identified by or to infect each other: the beginning of life, its end and everything in between. They were the story of all that had erotic potential once, but now, in the dim light of the early afternoon, were not much more than a symbol of the eternal sorrow he felt when thinking about what had brought him into this world.

'You should practise in front of a mirror how you come across in job interviews.'

Elin had been shaking her Pot Noodles when she imparted that precious wisdom in the kitchen the other day. Jimmie had never met anyone before who had to shake their Pot Noodles before making them, as if there were a better way of doing it than by following the instructions printed on its side. A more sophisticated way that didn't betray your lower instincts, that allowed you to believe that you were not sitting in the communal kitchen of a call centre on the sixth floor of a sad office block in a cheap part of town.

'It's important to know how people perceive you, to put yourself in their position. Even for non-acting jobs.'

Jimmie could just about see the kitchen door from where he was sitting now, and whenever he looked at it he could hear Elin's voice and smell all the food that had died in the microwave with the broken handle. Most things in here had gone yellow with too much human contact and were made from material that inspired self-hatred. It was in the kitchen that they spent most of their time together, and he never told her that to him her words smelled of old Tupperware. He didn't need those tainted words to know that their job was the opposite of acting. Elin and Jimmie were faceless people sweating in their cheap hoodies and trousers made by people not so different from themselves. People without daylight and dignity. And all around him were individuals from different parts of Europe using their languages to help run an international travel booking agent. They were the only international team in the building, made up mostly of

Europeans that sounded to the unsuspecting ear like they were French, German, Swedish, Italian or Spanish – but who often didn't look the part because their parents had emigrated from elsewhere.

The same was true for many of the English-language teams: the call centre was the perfect hiding place for all those who looked different, where they could work without offending the sensitivities of the dominant aesthetic. Reduced to their voices, they could do no harm. Jimmie often felt like one of the Seven Dwarfs, working in a rotten mine about to collapse and kill him while he was trying in vain to attract the attention of the princes above ground. In the end he would be left with no option but to fuck somebody as ugly as himself somewhere down in the darkness they were forced to share. Because the story never allowed for a prince to be pleasured by seven little men and nobody appreciated how much he cared for knights in shining armour. For two boys sharing a white horse. Maybe Jimmie should start shaking his food before eating it. Maybe it was all about inventing your own standards – making others believe that you could only ever be buried in a glass coffin, that the world had to care about what got stuck in your throat.

Elin was right that his drama school degree had never got him beyond appearing as a clown at children's parties together with Daniel or acting the part of the non-distinct Southern European relative at one of John Nobes's funeral services. Nobes had put up an ad at Jimmie's old drama school, and since no one else's parents were poor enough to force them to reply, he had had to make do with the chubby Italian boy. What did he want with a pale boy anyway, now that the city had become so foreign he could hardly recognize it? As it turned out, the Mediterranean complexion and the curly hair were quite versatile. Jimmie could occasionally even be hired out to one of the Jewish funeral places further north. Nobes had seemed content with his modern decision and hired Jimmie on a job-by-job basis as a mourning relative from abroad to liven up poorly attended funerals, a service the business had been offering for three generations with varying success. Nobes himself looked like his entire family had died from an overdose of processed cheese. Jimmie always wondered how English people's skin could get so pale that it took on the same colour as their hair and the food they put in front of them – why were they so frightened of eating anything that wasn't beige?

Now, as he could hear Wolf brush invisible crumbs off his desk and noticed the call light flash on his telephone, he regretted that he had lost that job, thanks to his mother, who, after all these years, had rediscovered her own body and decided to leave her bedroom to find herself a lover. Because she had to find a way into his space and touch his limits as if they were the cheap ends of a public monument, there for everyone to rub until they reached those layers of skin that look fresh but don't bleed. Red like a butcher's pride. Her own performance of sadness had outdone him with such force that he called it brutal sometimes, and as if that wasn't enough, it had landed him in this place where humiliation came in so many shades and colours that he often felt like a lost piece of glitter in a perverted kaleidoscope.

He missed those rides in the passenger seat of Nobes's hearse, the comfort of the worn leather seats and the dignity of their endeavour. He sometimes liked to imagine that he could have been born into it, that he really could have been the third generation to emerge from behind the discreet curtains of the funeral parlour. The man sitting next to him could always have been there and all the different things he felt for him could have been justified. The good and the bad. It's easier to dismiss the relationships we are born into, and Jimmie liked to imagine what it would be like to take someone's love for granted. That's why he missed those moments when they decided how sad he had to look that day or which part of the world his sadness was supposed to come from. All by himself, Jimmie felt overwhelmed by the task of having to navigate his own emotions and the sadness that now welcomed him every morning when he opened his eyes and realized that this life was really his own and not that of a long-lost Greek brother or an illegitimate Bulgarian son. That there was never anything other than his own heart to rely on.

'Thank you for waiting. My name is Jimmie. How can I help you today?'

'There's an issue with the infinity pool.'

'Are you in the Maldives by any chance?'

'How do you know?'

'They are famous for their infinity pools, sir.'

'But they are not giving everyone fair access to it and every time I go there is a queue.'

'What about the sea? I'm sure there's plenty of space at the beach.'

'That won't do.'

'Because the sea is finite?'

'Are you trying to be funny? I paid a lot of money for this holiday, and I want it to look right. Beach photos are much harder and not really my kind of thing. Have you ever tried to make a beach look expensive?'

'I'm afraid not. I'm rather cheap in general.'

Jimmie was longing to escape back to his orange cubicle and to feel his nerves calm down to the sound of the flushing toilet, to be away from all the voices and their greedy tongues. Away from their obsession with islands that would soon be swallowed by the sea because of their ridiculous lifestyles.

'You should try coming here one day. Have a bit of bubbly and make everyone jealous with your Insta account.'

'I think I can actually hear the sea in the background.'

'That's because I'm standing outside in the bloody queue. And by the time it's my turn, the light won't be as good and the guy from the hotel won't be up for taking pictures any more.'

'Is the pool so small that it can only accommodate one person?'

'No, but you want to be alone in there, make it look exclusive. Otherwise it's just a pool by the sea.'

'Right.'

'You should suggest to the hotel that they implement a booking system. That would give everyone a chance to make the most of the scenery. But like this it's complete mayhem.'

'Are people putting acid into each other's sun cream?'

Jimmie could imagine the whole drama unfolding. Gone were the years of simply reserving a spot by leaving your good German towel there and torturing a few unsuspecting friends with your slide shows once you were back. This was much more immediate, a world that no longer made sense on its own terms and had to be seen through artificial eyes.

'Look, I was merely suggesting a way to improve levels of satisfaction around here, but you clearly don't seem to care about that.'

'I sometimes suffer from what experts call a sudden loss of empathy. I'm like a heart that needs constant resuscitation.'

'You should find someone to sort you out. Can't imagine you have many happy customers.'

'And yet happiness is such a warm gun.'

'Twat.'

Jimmie looked at the picture of the hotel in the Maldives that he could never afford. It was one of those endless hotels with a perfect beach location, perfect staff and infinity pools, whose perverse purpose was to make people with money feel good. As he could still hear the sound of the sea in his mind, he started to visualize the other bits. The landscapes that had been violated to build these facades, the habitats that had to budge, the creatures we deemed unimportant in our relentless desire to appear like we have achieved something. To return with a better body, tanned, relaxed – and ideally well fucked. Entire countries depended on this desire, and they'd had to sacrifice all that was beautiful so that others could fly in and lie on a beach. Suddenly the world seemed so small to Jimmie and, though he mostly travelled vicariously on the screen in front of him, he couldn't shake the suspicion that there wasn't much left but images of these idyllic locations from which people returned with the illusion of an experience, because even the last bits of wilderness had been arranged to please the eye of some mindless lens. Concrete was simply another form of violence. And so, while he could still hear the waves, Jimmie dreamed of plants fighting their way through the endless swimming pool tiles, those cheap mosaics being destroyed one bit at a time, thousands of little green limbs reaching up until they were united with the sun. Until they could grow over that which was built to torment them.

The sound of the sea faded, and Jimmie emerged from behind the low, stained grey wall until he was high enough to find his situation drawing wrinkles on Wolf's forehead. It wasn't clear whether he had ever had hair.

'They used one of your calls during the meeting this morning, Jimmie.'

'Should I feel honoured?'

'You should be worried. Especially since your calls seem even stranger today.'

'Today is a special day, and I'm just keeping Simon's new number two busy. He needs to practise his management skills.'

'I always thought you were rather fond of Daniel.'

'Have you seen him without his hoodie yet?'

'Yes, he was there at the meeting. He looked very neat.'

'Everyone's beautiful when they're naked.'

Wolf shook his head and turned away, leaving Jimmie at the mercy of his next caller.

'Thank you for waiting. My name is Jimmie. How can I help you today?'

'I hate that woman in your commercial.'

'Excuse me?'

'That woman with the funny voice. I have to switch channel every time she comes on.'

'That's unfortunate.'

'Why did you have to pick one with such an annoying voice? How am I meant to enjoy that? And anyway, I prefer them with no space between their legs, nice round thighs with something to grab onto.'

A limp and soggy dick on a couch somewhere, unable to lift itself above layers of unwashed cotton and despair. Jimmie could feel its unrelenting softness, like the dangling limbs of a dead bird, and all the claims that came with a failed erection. The smell of unwashed skin, the taste of an unwanted body.

'Have you tried turning the sound off?'

'I wish I could do that with my own wife, turn the sound off. Always the same stories and nothing happening in the old bedroom any more…'

'I'm not sure what to advise here, sir. You're through to the official customer service centre, not couples therapy. We're here either to help people who want to make a booking or, in my case, if they have trouble with their holidays. But we're not responsible for any of the external content.'

'… and then you turn on the telly to have a bit of fun and they pick a skinny one with a terrible squeak and one of those ridiculous sun hats.'

'I understand, but —'

'Mind you, you've got quite a nice voice yourself. And I bet you're nice and round. Why don't you keep talking a bit for me.'

'I really don't think —'

'That's right. Just a little longer.'

Jimmie took off his headset as the breathing at the other end got deeper. He closed his eyes, but he could still hear the sound coming from the dirty little foam cushions. A pulse where there was supposed to be silence.

'Are you all right, Jimmie?'

'Yes, Wolf, sorry. It's a weirdo, just give me a minute.'

'Would you like me to take over?'

Jimmie nodded as Wolf smiled, and he felt his own breathing return to normal as he listened to the assassination of another man's pleasure.

It was in situations like these that he found Wolf's accent almost endearing. You couldn't hold a machine gun with a straight face while speaking Italian, but you could commit almost any atrocity using those endless rows of consonants that sounded like no poetry had ever occupied the spaces in between. Was it the language that made their fascism so much more severe? That allowed them to perfect the monster his own people had invented? Had that cluster of unfuckable sounds that they could never hide and that had come to haunt them – like a razor blade in a cake – inspired those famous genocidal urges and driven them to try and exterminate the Jews and their more melodic ways, in the same way nobody was allowed to have fun at a party where the host couldn't dance?

But then he envied Wolf for being so rooted in his culture that he couldn't even try to be anything else, and Jimmie always pictured him growing up in some healthy mountain community somewhere in the Alps. In touch with all the soil and tradition that the place had to offer, foretelling the weather by the size of the birds in the sky. Wolf surely had no idea what it was like to be dragged to another country as a child by your mourning mother, never to return. Nor what it felt like when your mother became that country where you had once lived, where you'd had a life and something like a family. The way she had become his only access to that place, its language and its food. Wolf wouldn't know what it was like when the people in the new country whose language you'd had to learn, to digest and make part of yourself, saw nothing but the good bits about your culture. The fucking dolce vita that you were meant to carry with you wherever you went, the less stuck-up version of themselves that you were meant to represent. The way they turned you into a vision of their own comfort, a space for projections of an imaginary country. They didn't understand that this had nothing to do with you, that all you knew were your mother's sad eyes and that strange dialect she had raised you in. That you were not fully formed but had been away for long enough to know that there was no life in the other country for you to return to, nothing to hold on to, nothing between those two worlds for you to float on and no mirror able to reflect what you actually saw in your mind. The reality he felt but never found portrayed outside himself. And yet it had never felt like his mother wanted to live in either of those countries; she didn't seem to want to live anywhere but this strange place within. The Signora had always lived at the centre of a maze, each turn a variation of her grief and Jimmie forever lost, unable to turn the right corner and find the way that would have allowed him to slay the beast she shared her labyrinth with.

'You might want to answer that call, Jimmie.' Helena floated past him, gently moving her fingers through his hair but not stopping for a chat. She was famous on the floor because she had a secret way of identifying the mystery caller, which made her almost impermeable to Simon's methods. Her calls were never dissected during the early meetings and so the world was mostly a prop to her, something that was there to make her look better until the next curtain call. Even though she was a member of Jimmie's team, where she talked Spanish and Catalan customers out of their misery, she never left the stage of the musical theatre on which she appeared in her dreams. The one thing she desired was for the thick velvet curtains to give way to her glorious shapes, and she didn't care about the darkness that surrounded every light. Jimmie had always liked the idea of being some winged glitter creature in her little universe of bodies and bliss. Of enjoying the freedom of those who are wanted and not the sharp edges of those who want. Of pretending that what had happened in the orange toilet last Friday hadn't made him feel even further away from the sun.

Helena was beautiful despite the hoodie, which she usually wore like an open jacket or even left hanging on her chair, making sure people wouldn't miss those surprisingly perfect breasts that she'd worked so hard for. Jimmie loved her enthusiasm, how she believed this job was only temporary, that it would one day be a mere anecdote to entertain people with at a comfortable dinner party. To her, the future wasn't just an illusion. And like a willing cat would purr when in pain, Jimmie momentarily deluded himself that this was a happy occasion. And like a good pet, he went to fetch his call.

'Thank you for waiting. My name is Jimmie. How can I help you today?'

'It's an emergency!'

'Can you please tell me where you are, madam, so that I can find the right numbers for the local ambulance and police services for you?'

'Don't be silly. I haven't lost a kidney. This emergency involves a cat.'

A grey cat with white paws and a big belly and those large blue eyes. The softest fur. Jimmie thought of Henry, rolling around on the pavement outside his house. He could hear his little meow which sounded like a lament.

'What happened to him?'

'You'd better be asking what happened to me. This is meant to be a luxury hotel, but I won't be giving you a good review, that's for sure.'

'There was an incident involving a cat at your hotel?'

'It's really a very simple story.'

Jimmie could picture a white holiday outfit in a Sicilian hotel lobby. He could sense the heat and the expectation of special treatment. He could taste the sweetness of those heavy southern desserts and the possibility of something like a memory. Something special. Waiters who made you feel warm inside and sunshine that would rejuvenate what had long been a lost cause. Perhaps even a hand to hold or a few seconds of a stranger's undiluted attention.

'And then I saw this cat coming towards me. I really don't mind cats, I'm not a pet hater or anything like that.

I would never put a cat in a bin like that crazy woman. And I thought this one looked friendly, but when I leaned over to pet his little head he turned around and sprayed all over my suitcase. It's a soft-shell one and now everything is soaked in cat piss – I didn't know they had that much fluid inside them. He even got me on my leg.'

Jimmie saw the loneliness she had brought with her in that suitcase and the hope of exchanging it for something better. And now there was nothing left but the end of all romance in the Mediterranean, no charming local to rescue her, a furry villain disappearing among his kin outside the lobby. Muttering spiteful Sicilian dialect in his stride. Little did she know that the cat had saved her from getting stuck with one of those Sicilian men who didn't age well and always complained about the quality of their food.

'I think we should take the cat's circumstances into consideration. I'm kind of Italian myself and I know that these cats often find themselves in very difficult situations. Many have been driven from their homes by vicious relatives, especially mothers. They're lonely and confused. Struggling to make it through the winter. It looks to me like this act of vandalism was really a cry for help. Most violence is just inhibited tenderness, and he was probably just hungry.'

'You think I should go and look for him?'

'Cat food is called *mangiare per i gatti* in Italian.'

'What if I don't find him?'

'Then you'll find another one. There are plenty of lost hearts if you look for them, and whoever saves a life saves the world.'

Jimmie loved those smart Jewish lines, and despite everything he was grateful to Daniel for sharing them, as they always put him in the mood for growing a beard and looking wise. If only his mother had known about them too, about mercy and the sanctity of all beating hearts. He would never forgive her for what she'd done to his little cat. His Henry. The only creature apart from Daniel he had enjoyed being imperfect with. The Signora never tired of complaining that Henry had often been sick in her shoes and that recently he had started to leave delicate cat poo stains on the sofa and once, during one of those new occasions when she actually left her bedroom, even on her pillow. He and Henry had both been shocked when, after all those years, the woman who'd managed to turn London into an Italian village started to leave her one-mile radius, spurred on by sudden desire. Even though she felt she had to go and be with her lover at odd hours for fear of imaginary gossip, proof that she had never left her motherland behind. It was just the story she liked to tell herself while she was secretly still craving the outrage her adopted country was not prepared to offer – the best an immigrant could hope for was silence.

She couldn't understand that Henry, too, had felt abandoned. Unable to compete with where her heart had gone, it was his way of finding her attention and ultimately his own fate. Jimmie had never shared her approach to animals, all that self-involved brutality she'd inherited from her mother that left no space for the softer moments but instead reduced these poor creatures to their mere functions. To the advantage you could gain from their flesh and fur. Since she couldn't turn poor Henry into one of his grandmother's old fur hats, she mostly ignored him, leaving him to carry his little heart behind her like a piece of prey. Sometimes Jimmie could see himself in Henry, a hopelessly fat person trying to offer a heart that looked like a dead rat to others. He was sure that if his mother had stayed in Italy, she would have grown a hunch going around neighbouring villages to drown unwanted kittens in a bucket in exchange for a chat and a nice glass of local wine.

He closed his eyes. When he opened them he saw the shiny black keyboard in front of him. He knew that the cleaner never touched it, that there was probably a different pandemic lurking beneath each letter – he had worked enough late shifts to learn about this open betrayal. The obvious gap in Simon's desire for control. All the cleaner ever did was empty the bins and use the special key to drink free hot chocolate from the vending machine. All the others had to pay for their so-called Italian coffee, anything to remind them that this was not a regular office with free tea and biscuits but some version of the future that could only be described as hell, though with less drama and none of the kinky stuff. No orgies with frozen tears and no eternity because, unlike other employees, they were never granted the consolation that their suffering would last forever. The beauty of the zero-hours contract meant they could get fired any day, even during their shifts. Like the skinny French guy with the intense look on his face who was sent home the other day for watching porn during working hours.

Jimmie had felt for him. It was hard to imagine that anyone would want to fuck someone called Quentin; the urge to touch himself must have been overwhelming. Jimmie had never enquired whether the film in question had been French, or whether Quentin had deigned to derive pleasure from another language. What if it had been one of those glitzy LA productions? Now the angry god of French arrogance and contempt would send him to a purgatory especially designed for those proud bearers of the most important language on earth, who had fallen from grace by wanking to those undignified foreign vowels, who shouted *yes* instead of *oui*. Jimmie liked the idea of Quentin in his very own purgatory, having to look at American tourists in berets and striped shirts, forced to eat orange English cheese and wear a German outfit. Preferably one that involved leather and a stupid hat with a feather because, like most French people, he deserved his fate.

The cleaner, the disgruntled Portuguese husband of a disgruntled Portuguese wife, had managed to steal a copy of the special key and was now bleeding the company dry without getting as much as a warning. Earlier on Jimmie had considered asking him for a free hot chocolate in exchange for his silence, but one look at the man's face while he was holding the hoover like a kendo stick had taught him enough to mind his own business, to pretend not to notice when he heard the machine gurgle with the sweet hot milk.

The phone seemed to be ringing again, but with Helena off to buddy the newbies and Wolf using his five-minute break to determine how far up Simon's arse he could get by demonstrating his famous German efficiency, Jimmie was suddenly unsure what was actually happening. He no longer knew where his body ended and where the world began, because the sound of the telephone had started to follow him around like an army of possessive thoughts. His job had invaded his body, and it became impossible for him to tell where the part of himself he was supposed to own began and when he was merely brushing against the cage he was forced to work in. Who owned his limbs when he woke up on a Sunday at six, only to be haunted by the telephone's red button flashing in front of him like a group of red demons doing a round dance, their oversized genitalia competing with the first rays of sunshine? Where was he when he could hear the phone's subtle ringtone while trying to fit under the blanket his grandmother had knitted all those years ago? It all happened inside him, and it didn't matter where he was because he couldn't stop seeing it all – at night, in the morning, when he tried not to be lonely, on the bus that took him to work like a despondent whale, in the entrance hall that looked like the sad part of an airport, inside the lift that took him in and sucked him up. The lift that might one day crash and push his feet into his head thanks to some laws of physics he didn't understand.

Then the inevitable arrival, the noise of hundreds of voices competing with their own failures. The pain of signing in too late and not getting paid for the first hour because the bus had been delayed that day. The atmosphere of a school playground, his inability to get laid written on every face. His old fears singing as he tried to find his pod, as he walked past all those eyes as vacant as those of a cat finding relief on your mother's best pillow. It was all there, no matter where he went: he was always in that lift, his body sold for minimum wage and no sick pay. Work had become another fluid in his body, and some day he would be riddled with ailments and as ugly as the chair he was sitting on.

And still the phone kept flashing.

'Thank you for waiting. My name is Jimmie. How can I help you today?'

'I'm in that fancy hotel in Munich, something with Bavarian in the title.'

'Sounds like you have chosen an excellent location.'

'I don't care about the location. Or this city with all those old Nazis in fur coats. I care about the room.'

Jimmie often ignored the rules and googled people while talking to them, but in this case he didn't need to. He could tell that she had the same wrinkles between her breasts as his mother, that most treacherous sign of age. Skin gone soft and tired. Unlike his mother, she wore her body with pride, and in his mind she spoke with a pair of those perfectly fake lips that Helena had paid for with the last of her savings. This woman didn't obey those ancient laws of fertility and shame that would have forbidden her from finding pleasure beyond the good years of reproductive purpose, like a smelly old priest in a dirty robe, hiding skin they feared would tempt the gods. This voice was different, free from the dark layers his mother couldn't live without.

'Is it not to your satisfaction?'

'That's quite the word. The people here are lovely and not too German, but the room is orange.'

'Orange?'

'Yes, orange. Even the toilet paper smells of peach.'

A shrill orange like the make-up on Helena's face when seen from beneath in the bathroom light? Or an unattainable orange like the sunset on that fake photo above the downstairs reception desk designed to distract from the security guard's unforgiving features? Perhaps a rusty orange like the fading golden letters above John Nobes's funeral parlour? It was hard to imagine the setting of this complaint.

'And orange is not a good colour?'

'Depends on your preferences. I can't really get in the mood if the colours are all wrong.'

'Does it bring back memories of ginger nuts?'

Her laughter was full of the kind of confidence he wished his mother had found for herself.

'It's just that I've had a long day and I wish I could relax a little.'

'And you can't change the room?'

'They're all orange.'

'It sounds like you're in one of those fast-food chains where they use aggressive colours to discourage people from staying too long.'

'You mean they're doing this deliberately to make sure people keep their hands above the blanket? You think it's a Catholic thing?'

'I wouldn't know, madam. I'm not a priest, nor a nun. To be honest with you, I haven't even been baptized, but I know that they chose orange as a colour for our toilets here for much the same reason.'

'But that's not the right place to feel like yourself. Always stay precious.'

Jimmie tried to smile against the sharper corners of his memories.

'Would you like me to try to cancel your booking?'

'Don't worry. I'll pretend I'm a lonely nun. Just promise me that you'll treat yourself to something better than that orange toilet, will you?'

His reply was more of a nod, his voice silenced under this sudden care that felt like a mother had stroked his hair. A gesture he had always longed for, like a needy pet. As a child, he had insisted the Signora wash his hair. He claimed that it required conditioner and that he was afraid of the tears it caused whenever he tried to do it on his own. The joy he'd felt the few times she'd agreed, when he sat in the scratched old bathtub and she sat on the edge, massaging the apple-scented shampoo into his hair while he held a wet flannel to his face to protect his eyes. All the sensations as warm and trusting as the water she used to wash his curls, his head tilted back slightly, felt like a loving embrace. He could still taste the water as it dripped from the wet cloth into his smiling mouth, and he liked to think that she had smiled back at him in that mouldy bathroom where he wished he could have stayed, forever comforted by a world he couldn't see.

Jimmie looked around him and wondered if he could blame the state of the carpet beneath him for his own dysfunctions, but the dying colours seemed wildly indifferent to his claims. There were no responsibilities to be found in this eternal ugliness of a pretend office where even their language was a poor attempt at a corporate reality that would never be reflected in their weekly pay cheques.

Without having to turn his head, Jimmie could feel that Wolf had been listening.

'What do you mean you haven't been baptized – aren't you Italian?' He looked at him with the honest curiosity of a narrow mind.

'Kind of. But it wasn't possible to get a baptism with my name.'

'Why not?'

'Because back then in my village you could only get baptized by our Catholic priest if you chose the Italian name of a saint. And I believe the Holy Jimmie didn't make it into their books.'

'I always thought that your name was a bit strange. I presumed it was a nickname.'

'No, it's my real name. Not a lubricant to make things easier for other people.'

'It's not very typical, you know?'

'I know. I'm not called Giuseppe or Massimo and I'm not Catholic. It's a lot to take in.'

'So you're not actually Italian. That explains it.'

Jimmie pulled his hood over his head and stared at his old nail varnish. The chipped dark blue now seemed unsuitable and he longed for something fresher, a shade of light green or even a soft violet. A colour that knew all about spring and its secrets, that felt like floating in clear water with the trees outlining the sky above. He was unsure what Wolf had suddenly understood about him that he had never managed to understand himself. The weird German talked as if a law of nature had chosen to reveal itself in this very moment, to drop its pants and show everyone what it was really about. As if a piece of wisdom had just fallen from the tree and landed straight on his ugly egghead and now it was clear why Jimmie's own culture was often a mystery to him. Why he'd never understood how – if not to stir people's fantasies by having a handsome young man in their private rooms – Jesus had saved the world by being miserable and naked on a piece of wood. Or why Italians all wore the same puffa jacket in winter and how it was possible to perform an identity he didn't fully possess. How he had failed so miserably at being his mother's son.

What is a country anyway, Jimmie wondered as he looked across the busy desks with all the different languages floating around them, the murmur of their words doing a dance like innumerable little birds. Formations that were beautiful but would never reveal all their secrets, a dance their tongues were born with that made them recognize their wings and marvel at each other's steps and turns. Was each of these flocks a country? Jimmie liked the idea of himself as a fat bird trying to dance alongside those he wasn't born with while his own flock slowly disappeared over the horizon, taking their signs with them. He knew it was possible to dance with other birds, that nobody ever understood every single word they said because words tasted different in every mouth. A flock was only a flock when seen from below, otherwise it was just your life. Jimmie knew that the best moments were those with your feet above the ground: a space where nobody had a country, like waking up without knowing where you were. No language was fully known, no tongue without variation. No country a reality beyond the borders of our imagination.

He stood up to stretch and could feel the lower part of his belly slip out from under his T-shirt and start rubbing against the inside of the company hoodie. Like everything he had ever worn, it was too tight for him, another reminder that there would never be an oversized look for him, that his body had never been a source of joy. He would never be able to walk like Helena, with that fierce confidence of someone who could get any prince, priest or mother to fuck them. Looking at Helena now, as she told the new French guy at the pod next to the one he shared with Wolf how to embrace the true meaning of customer service without watching porn at work, nobody would have thought that she had set out as a rich girl from Catalonia, destined to take over the family's pork production empire and to marry a neat man with slender limbs from an equally good family. Helena was meant to be some sort of local pig queen, raised on soil that had grown infertile with all the excess blood, the animal hearts that outnumbered those of their human tyrants, and she had decided to stage a revolt in their stead. She had been disowned by her parents after a rebellious stint in a Barcelona strip club. For looking like pleasure in the heat. She was no longer respectable but divine. She used her body to entertain others and became infected with that incurable love of the stage that made her eyes flicker even when she was pretending to be at work. And so she had gone abroad to work hard for her new curves and features, to change her name and humiliate her family by working like a cheap immigrant. Despite the occasional doubt that Jimmie was familiar with from all the other faces around him – the little twitch here and there, remnants of a world where you would never trade comfort and expensive fabrics for a vulgar ambition – he always sensed in Helena the pride of someone who had come out of the womb ready for an adventure.

'What are you after, Don Corleone? Do you need more chewing gum?'

'I was admiring your lipstick. That shade of red is wild, and you do it so perfectly.'

Helena smiled with that little grin that seemed to lift up her nose, and he couldn't tell whether her voice was tainted by gossip or whether she was still sitting on her treasure.

'It's all thanks to you for letting me use your beautiful lips. Practice makes perfect.'

'I can tell.'

'And look at you! Now you've got a taste for it yourself.'

'It's a special occasion.'

'Naughty Friday?'

The look in her eyes made him feel nervous.

'I have my reasons.'

'Do you want me to touch it up for you?'

'I'm not sure I'm free today.'

'We could use the ladies this time.'

'I'm sorry.'

'Make sure you don't take any sweets from strangers.'

As she turned away, Jimmie felt his body's regrets rushing across his mind and he was almost glad about his date with Simon. He was aware that Helena knew that, according to the hierarchy of bodies, he would never be able to take her down with him to the unglamorous world of unemployment. It was always the pretty people from first class who got a seat on the lifeboat, the bodies that had been well looked after. The traces of Helena's comfortable pig-money childhood were still there for everyone to see, and Jimmie knew, that faced with the same accusations, their bodies would experience rather different consequences. He tried to pull his T-shirt back over his belly without anyone noticing and sat back at his desk.

'Jimmie. Could you please take this call for me and tell them to wait? My digestion seems somewhat overactive today.' Wolf didn't even wait for his answer and rushed to the toilet, the arse wipes most likely hidden in a secret neck pouch underneath his hoodie.

He was about to be good and pick up when Simon signalled for him to take off his headphones and forced him to let the call drop back into the endless void of the callers' queue. Jimmie could almost hear a hapless German tourist scream as they were sucked back into the chaos of a lonely predicament – Wolf was the only German speaker on shift in the complaints section today and it would be a while before he considered himself clean enough to return to his desk. Though he had never followed him, Jimmie could tell that Wolf had exaggerated hygiene habits, that he was possibly even one of those maniacs who could only relieve themselves if they were completely naked.

'Have you cancelled your plans yet, Jimmie?'

Simon stood next to him now, one hand on the little wall that separated him from Wolf, the veins on his hands showing above his knuckles. Jimmie loved those fingers, and the way Simon would sometimes move them across his lips when he was lost in thought. Right now, nothing in his face suggested pink lipstick or a Swedish blowjob outside his parents' house. There was no satisfaction hidden in his features, just the rigour that Jimmie found so enticing.

'Sorry, I haven't spoken to Elin yet.'

'I really need to talk to you.'

'Is it that urgent?'

'Quite.'

'I guess I can always rearrange things with her. We were meant to hang out, it wasn't a date or anything like that.'

Simon didn't return Jimmie's smile. 'Please do. I'll come and find you after my shift and we can speak somewhere more private.'

There was something official about his body. As Simon returned to his desk with that perfectly straight back of his, Jimmie imagined him going through some files in a secret archive or signing someone's death warrant. When he thought about the dominance hidden in those fingers, he could feel his lips swelling and his eyes losing focus. His vowels tripped over each other as he tried to speak while imagining those fingers grabbing him firmly by the hair, making him do things he wasn't sure he wanted. Jimmie knew that it was rare but that miracles sometimes happened for fat people, and he briefly imagined that this was nothing but Simon's warped way of flirting in public – that Simon had realized that Jimmie had so much more to give than a healthy Scandi with a teenage fascination for neon who dreamed of life in a forest. To share some affection with an Italian could be as fresh and delicate as Botticelli's *Spring*.

It was mostly because of his strange obsession with Simon, that mix of fear and devotion, that Jimmie tried to do his job properly and didn't resort to consuming adult content at his desk. Or, even worse, to eating. Typical of all places that had no real interest in hygiene and a cleaner who regularly got high on stolen hot chocolate, the call centre had lots of hygiene regulations but, as with any place of official discomfort, they only enforced those rules that added to people's humiliation. If you were caught with a bag of crisps or one of Daniel's free granola bars, they told you off in front of the whole team and forced you to dispose of your edibles in the nearest bin or leave them on your supervisor's desk until the end of your shift, giving them free rein to contaminate your food with their spare body particles. Jimmie was more terrified of this kind of merry violence than of the dissection of his phone calls, and the thought of the entire team staring at his food and then at his body stopped him from keeping even cough drops in his bag. Instead, he always left his food in Elin's rucksack; her slender body was less at risk of being caught.

At least the employees of Vanilla Travels Ltd weren't treated as badly as the people in Wolf's stories. The other day he had told Jimmie that when he was still living in Germany, he had to sell newspaper and magazine subscriptions over the phone – a modern version of the old-fashioned door-to-door harassment of organized salespeople, charities and religions. Wolf had lived something like the life of a disgraced Avon lady, having to inflict pain in order to pay for his food. He targeted old people who would take out a seventeenth subscription to the same magazine in exchange for being able to talk to someone not on TV. Wolf's supervisors would get angry and spiteful if they didn't meet their targets, and once his colleague, a little man from Romania whose name Wolf had forgotten, was locked into the office all night as a punishment for not finding the right number of gullible pensioners, brought to their stiff knees by years of neglect. Jimmie often thought about the little man from Romania, whether he had maybe been called Alexandru or Bogdan, whether he had sometimes acted the part of one of his relatives and whether a similar incident, possibly involving a freezer or a refrigerator van, could have led to the loss of Wolf's toes.

'Did you take the call, Jimmie?'

'I'm sorry, Wolf. Simon asked me to get off the phone.'

'Let's hope this won't cause any problems with my ratings.'

'What are they going to do? Lock you up overnight?'

Wolf tried to smile, but in his face Jimmie could detect the fear of being hung up by his feet and beaten with old gossip magazines and broken telephone cables. The shadows that had followed him into his migration like unwanted relatives. Jimmie knew it was wrong to long for torture and that those stories deserved his full compassion and respect, yet the idea of being asphyxiated by Simon with his leather belt left him with a pleasant sensation between his legs.

'You might at least want to answer your own calls.'

He hated it when Wolf was in a sulk, their little island turned into a place of tension and discomfort.

'Thank you for waiting. My name is Jimmie. How can I help you today?'

'There is a hair on my pillow.'

'I'm sorry about that, madam. I imagine it's not yours?'

'Most certainly not. This one is long, dark and curly. I went grey a long time ago.'

'Seems like you've got a good eye for hair.'

'I caught my ex-girlfriend that way. That hair was also very different from my own.'

Jimmie started reaching for his own curls – they had never messed with anyone's fidelity, had never been a clue in one of those riddles of unleashed emotions. He could picture the pillow she was looking at, the kind of white you wish you could find in an English hospital but that only existed in hotels and those fantasy resorts that looked after fortunate bodies. The kind of white that seems to hold no secrets, that is not scared of memories because it has no way of holding on to them.

'I know this is not the point, but do you know what it's like to wake up on a Saturday morning after you have travelled for work all week and then you finally come home and realize there is a stranger's hair on your partner's pillow?'

'I'm afraid not, madam. I still live with my mother.'

'Those were the most ridiculous hours of my entire life.'

Jimmie could hear her swallowing back her tears, and he knew from his three-hour training session with Helena on how to handle escalations that when people were agitated it was best to just let them talk. No emotion lasts forever. For some reason the hair he could now picture on the woman's pillow was one of Helena's brightly coloured curls, that shade of red she always brought back from Barcelona which was so beautiful that everyone thought it was real. He could see it glowing crimson, and he could almost imagine the little curl smile with that swagger Helena had perfected at drama school. Suddenly Jimmie grasped the sadness of trying to nurse a broken heart in an unconvincing spa hotel on the outskirts of Prague.

'It's like everybody and everything is mocking me. For my wobbly arse, for my strange face, for the way I drink my tea. Everything about me has become ridiculous. But these are old-people problems. You're probably one of those young people who don't even believe in relationships any more.'

'I do believe in them, madam. I just don't get to practise them. And I know what you mean – it's hard to feel attractive on your own. But what about the room? Shall I ask them to change it for you?'

'I haven't found any other horrors. And the place is perfect for when you never actually intended to visit the city.'

'It was probably someone from housekeeping who wasn't careful with their hair. I'm sure they changed the sheets before you arrived.'

'But what shall I do with the hair?'

'Honestly?'

'Go on.'

'Keep it. Keep it and pretend you got to fuck someone extraordinary. Nothing wrong with believing in your own story.'

Her giggle told him that it was safe to leave her alone in the company of a Czech chambermaid's stranded hair.

He leaned back in his chair, a squeaking thing without armrests that barely supported his weight, the cheap green fabric worn out by the traces of other people's anxieties. Armrests were only for Simon and now Daniel, their team leader and his assistant, proud owners of basic comfort. Jimmie leaned back a little more, feeling the plastic that was trying to resist his body about to snap. He couldn't tell whether Daniel was at his new desk, hidden from view by several screens which gave him access to everybody's performances. Little graphs growing from scratch every day, like zombies' fingers rising in a cemetery, but at least one of these pathetic lines would have Jimmie's name on it and he was content that Daniel would have to stare at those six letters from now on.

Jimmie didn't want Daniel to think that he was looking for him, or to reveal his brightly coloured lips – the shade he'd chosen for him – too soon. He was keen to go and talk to the other Israeli guys, Daniel's friends from the veg box team who were popular for working the Christian holiday shifts and who got just as high on gossip as the Italians.

Even Simon sometimes went over there to have a chat, especially since they were all going after the same tight-lipped shiksa. Jimmie had picked up that word at one of the Jewish funerals that Mr Nobes had rented him out to. It suited Elin so perfectly. She always looked as though all her ancestors had been Viking-loving blondes who gave birth to blue-eyed children with translucent skin that would make any Nazi giddy with delight. The Israeli guys were bound to know whether Elin's date with Simon had been a success, whether this time she'd got lucky and found someone who was willing to commit to her vision of a good life.

Daniel's friend, whose name Jimmie kept forgetting, had never been willing to take his feelings for Elin seriously until he ruined their only date by failing to appreciate the importance of having a term for the female equivalent of wanker. Of Elin being a proud wankeress. Jimmie could relate; they were like fifteenth-generation Italians abroad who preferred to keep things in the family and only occasionally fucked a forbidden fruit. Jimmie had always felt at home during those Jewish funerals, where nobody had ever contested his descent from the Holy Land. After all, Italy had enough ports to claim almost any heritage. He loved wearing the little skullcap while listening to their sad vowels and, even though he had never made it to a shiva, he had never felt excluded the way he did by Daniel's habits. He never felt like a forbidden fruit and, if he had been slimmer, he might have ripped open his shirt upon hearing of his mother's death. Sadly, she refused to die, and his chest wasn't a thing worthy of display; the reluctant hair around his nipples seemed to prove he was not destined to become a hairy Mediterranean man like Daniel, whose skin was forever protected by his very own fur coat. Perhaps his system had adjusted to his early removal from his native soil and his body hair felt as alienated as his tongue; Jimmie had long blamed this on the lack of a divine presence in the food they ate on this island. It must have been the reason why his body hadn't developed the way it would have done in the other country, where according to his mother even the last rotten tomato had a personality, a set of colours that made you feel alive.

Wolf was still mourning his call rating, so Jimmie signalled to Simon to get permission to get up and walk across the floor, past the strange Danish man and towards the brighter world of the booking team to find Elin. She had the kind of personality that allowed her always to get the same desk at the same pod, basking in daylight like the born leader of a chicken coop; she was always on top of the ladder with the other Scandis, close to their team's one big window. Her headset always looked fresh and even her chair seemed less crippling than his own, as though it were made from superior material. Jimmie often wondered how she had ended up in this place, why she had left a place as perfect and pretty as Sweden. As he approached her desk, he could already tell that she was biting the inside of her cheeks while staring at her inbox, and the way her lips were moving made her look like she was about to turn into something else, an animal trying to wriggle out of an old coat, a Transformer stuck in its final motions. The more she chewed the more Jimmie expected her whole body to follow and start shaking with the same square-shaped movements. The sharp, almost rectangular line of her jaws reminded Jimmie of the aesthetics of his first Game Boy, and he couldn't help humming some of its tunes. Had Elin made Pac-Man noises as she approached Simon's cock with her pink lips? Or had their bodies given off those crushing Tetris sounds as they fucked in the toilet cubicle behind the downstairs bar? Had their limbs started to disappear with every instance of their successful union?

'Are you already taking your break? I thought we'd said six. You know I can't stay very long.'

Elin never took her headphones off for these short conversations but only pushed the microphone a little further down, while the other Scandis looked at him like he was a greedy fox about to pounce on something that deserved to live.

'I just came over because I can't make it any more. Simon asked me for a chat, and I couldn't really say no.'

'Oh really?' She stopped chewing. 'Did he say what it was about?'

'He only said that he wanted us to go somewhere more private. But this way you can go straight for your drinks.'

She smiled. 'Is that why you're wearing lipstick?'

'Oh, piss off, Elin. Will you ever stop stealing my lines?'

'Will you ever stop being such a bitch?'

'Fair enough.'

'Let me know how it goes.'

She pushed her microphone back up, and Jimmie understood that his audience was over. It was clear that Elin wouldn't tell him anything and that he would have to go and speak to Daniel's friends in their green hoodies to find out whether she'd had a chance to take those 1950s-style glasses off Simon's serious face.

Jimmie headed back to his lonely pod, the unsuccessful corner of the school playground where none of the beautiful bodies dared to mingle. He was walking as slowly as he could, enjoying the sensation of Simon's angry gaze sliding down his back, when Daniel appeared in front of him. Daniel's eyes were two shades lighter than his own – a strange kind of brown that looked like it had once been another colour. When he looked into those eyes, Jimmie was reminded why some people thought it was a blessing to blind animals in certain situations. Daniel, too, would have been better off not seeing all the things his heart couldn't bear.

'Jimmie, *hamud*. How are you?'

'I almost didn't recognize you there in your new outfit.'

'You look different too.'

Jimmie's voice had taken on an unfamiliar tone, more official, like Simon's. In another language, he would probably have switched to a formal register to hide the discomfort he felt beneath his new shirt.

'I'm surprised you would notice my beautiful new lips.'

'Jimmie.'

'Given your new importance.'

'Not in front of other people, please. It's my first day.'

Jimmie could see that irresistible hurt appear in Daniel's eyes, the pain only his pigments put together so beautifully.

'Of course not. We all know that you're a very private man.'

'Look —'

'Spare yourself the trouble. You don't have anything to fear from me, but I need to get back to my desk or else you might have to give me a warning.'

Jimmie tried to look busy, but he knew he was a lousy actor. Just as well he had mostly performed in front of dead people. He walked away without looking into Daniel's eyes again; he could feel the sadness from this morning returning, and he didn't want him to notice it.

'*Ach*, Jimmie. There is a call that's been waiting for you for a few minutes and I thought that you would be keen to deal with it yourself.'

Wolf always sounded like a cheap version of Count Dracula when he tried to be gleeful, and Jimmie figured that peace between them had been restored.

'Thanks for the heads-up, Wolf.' Jimmie sat down, almost relieved to see nothing but the flashing red button. 'Thank you for waiting. My name is Jimmie. How can I help you today?'

'They are not allowing us to be naked here. They claim that this is a family hotel.'

'And are you currently dressed?'

'I thought it was safe to be naked on the balcony while my wife is taking a little nap.'

Jimmie tried hard to resist the images the comfortable middle-aged voice brought up, but it was clingy like a wet shower curtain. At this point he almost preferred the rude voices to those that drew him into the warmth of their sunlit hotel rooms during those late afternoons when tourists tried to fuck in preparation for dinner and other so-called entertainments. He felt tempted to hang up and hide in the toilet until the nudist couple in the family hotel had been dealt with by someone else.

'And how can I help?'

'My wife and I, we care about our tan, if you know what I mean?'

'I'm afraid I don't.'

'Seamless. That's what we are after. A seamless tan, front and back and bottom in particular. But now we have been told by the hotel manager that we cannot be naked in the pool area because of the children. And there isn't even a nudist beach nearby.'

Jimmie felt a slight nausea creeping up his throat. He had to force his eyes to stay open to help him resist this onslaught of unwanted intimacy which had only found its way to him via a combination of numbers and fate. The strange system of codes and buttons that connected people all over the world, made everyone available via cables that lay at the bottom of the ocean. The world felt so small, yet

Jimmie took comfort in that image, his voice somewhere down there in the impenetrable darkness of the deep blue sea, an eternity of freedom between him and the other end. A whole world of undiscovered creatures that he remembered as he thought about his date with Simon. The possible end of his career as a call boy now seemed like a sudden ray of sunlight in an underwater forest, a first hint that he could go and join the undiscovered creatures if he wanted to. There would be space for him in the darkness below.

'I'm not sure how best to describe it, but we're a fairly mainstream booking agent. We don't cater to such special needs.'

'Are you trying to say that my wife and I have special needs? We're not asking for step-free access.'

'No, sir, I just meant that we don't offer any "special" holidays in our programme – no nudism, no tantra classes, no butterfly taxidermy and no escape rooms or anything like that.'

'So you think I'm a pervert?'

'I never said that. I was merely trying to explain our company policy to you. Your request is simply a bit too niche for us. Plus we always advise our customers to check their hotel requirements before booking.'

'But we're here now. What do you want us to do?'

'I would imagine they sell swimwear at reception or down by the beach. Or else you might want to try wearing a sock?'

'These are legitimate concerns, and I really don't appreciate your tone.'

Jimmie couldn't help but mute the conversation for a bit. Wolf was staring at him as he burst into tears of laughter for the first time in days. He had never understood why it was important to be tanned when being naturally dark-skinned was met with so much hostility. And the idea of some English guy with a cheap white tennis sock on his cock walking around a family resort in Sardinia trying to get a tan his skin could never retain was too much to bear. It took him almost a minute to compose himself.

'I'm sorry, but I had to discuss this with my colleague from the holiday resort department. While we are also greatly concerned about the tan lines on your bottom, I'm afraid there is nothing we can do apart from advising you to buy swimwear or to spend your holiday indoors. My colleague tells me that you can also get tanned through a glass window – just don't stand too close or the children might be able to see you. We hope you enjoy the rest of your holiday.' He hung up before Muppet-cock could say anything else.

'I almost forgot to mention that Daniel was trying to find you during your last break.'

Wolf obviously thought it best not to discuss this sudden outburst of humour in case it returned. Each little silence was a reminder that uncontrollable laughter was the stain of the anarchic.

'Did he say what he wanted?'

'No. I fear that he wanted to look at pictures of your dog again.'

'My dog was a cat. And don't worry, we bumped into each other and there aren't any more pictures of Henry.'

'That's for the best. It's hardly suitable for a man like Daniel to spend so much time with you and your cat photos. And you can do better than that, you don't need to hide behind some silly pet.'

Wolf returned to his screen, leaving Jimmie feeling as if he had tripped over the hole where a tree used to live.

They had sometimes looked at pictures of Henry together, and Jimmie didn't care if Wolf thought that wasn't appropriate grown-up behaviour. What did he know, with his arse wipes and serious footwear? Growing up wasn't an option. When Jimmie thought about his future he couldn't see anything new; he could only see the same old things tainted by age and decay, his skin giving in to his weight. His lungs crushed under his chest and his salary still too small to afford a dishwasher. When he looked in the mirror, he didn't see the reflection of the kind of happy face his bank used to try to tempt him into debt, a face embodying stability and a state-approved relationship. They never chose the face of someone who continued to live with his mother, waiting for her death as the only hope for some independence. His was the face of someone who was envious of his own mother's face because even after years spent soaking in grief it could still attract romance.

Jimmie no longer felt like talking to Daniel about any of this, especially not the cat, but if he kept quiet, he might get away with pretending that nothing had ever happened. Knowing Daniel, he would just start saying motivational things to him again. He would remind him of the good times he thought they'd had when they'd performed as clowns for rich people's offspring. That this was a natural step in every actor's career. Daniel never mentioned that bodies like theirs rarely featured on screen, that they would never inspire commercially acceptable desires. Jimmie never wanted to think about that particular summer birthday party and those children again. He wasn't Mediterranean enough to share the enthusiasm, and he never got over the disappointment of how ugly these children were, a babycino crowd that looked like a hot-water bottle had given birth to them, little faces that already reeked of privilege and fatigue from too much choice. And he and Daniel in cheap clown costumes trying to fight the heat of that summer day. Jimmie was sure that Daniel had used his smile from the children's parties to get his new position, acting as if he was still wearing those thick layers of red and white clown make-up. But that summer day the heat had become a reality and Jimmie had discovered what lay beneath those layers. Away from it all, Daniel smiled like a lover who knew that love rarely existed in two minds at the same time, and Jimmie wished he had been able to appreciate the subtleties of this melancholia.

Bored as always, Jimmie reached into his pocket and found last week's chewing gum. Helena's little gift. And because he thought that temptation was a sign from God, Jimmie made use of the momentary afternoon lull to sneak into the kitchen and enjoy the call centre's most dangerous treat. The kitchen was only marginally less offensive than the toilet. It didn't smell of piss and unhappiness and there was a window in there, London visible in the distance, like a bride whose hand he would never get to hold. It was impossible to be alone in there because it was open to the entire floor, and there were always at least two people present he had never seen before, talking in a language he couldn't understand. Jimmie always wondered what had brought them here, why they had left their languages and mothers behind and decided to lay down roots over here. He smiled as he looked at the two women, holding old mugs between slender fingers, talking as if their lives mattered. He knew there was agency in living in an overpriced room abroad, a sense of delight in choosing to be miserable somewhere other than home and that, as long as it was your decision, you would find a way to cope. Those were the illusions brought about by the dignity of a susceptible mind, just like his mother had believed her heart could forever remain in one piece.

Jimmie always worried that the foldable plastic chairs would collapse under his weight, and so instead he leaned against the wall and looked out of the window into the last hours of a London day. Slowly placing the chewing gum on his tongue, he savoured the sweetness of this transgression and his thoughts turned to last Friday as the artificial flavour crawled across his tongue like a limbless creature.

'Are you ready for a little toilet break with me?'

Helena was smiling at Jimmie, pursing her lips as she spoke with that accent he was so fond of. When Spanish people spoke, he could always hear their tongues, and when Helena was on the phone to her friends in Catalan, Jimmie always thought of tiny helicopter blades rotating in her mouth, her tongue sounding so busy that he found it hard to focus. When she spoke in English, he could still hear her tongue tapping to the rhythm of her speech, her accent so much more subtle than his mother's heavy Italian endings.

'I'm always ready for you.'

'Let's go then. This is my last break for today. After that I have to dash and start preparing for tonight.'

Jimmie could tell that she was in her usual Friday mood; her body was shimmering in anticipation of the night. Since Helena had already defeated the mystery caller, Jimmie could ignore Simon and follow her perfectly shaped bum to the bathroom, where she had agreed to a lipstick tutorial to help him prepare for a casting. Or so he'd told her.

'Boys or ladies?'

'I'll follow your mood.'

'Let's both be boys then. There'll be less traffic in there even though Simon might interrupt us.'

She had taken him by the hand and pulled him behind her.

'Who knows? He might arrange for his own secret breaks here.'

'Simon? Don't be ridiculous. I'm sure the wildest thing he's ever done is imagine a girl putting a finger near his hole. I know the type – imagine him in ten years' time with his neat little wife and first signs of hair loss. There is really nothing exciting about him. These men never fuck outside their mother's front garden.'

'Have you tried?'

'Darling. Please.. What is it with you? Men have on average nine erections a day. You can't expect to be at the centre of all of them.'

He liked it when she spoke like an older sister and he briefly imagined a life in which such moments of tenderness didn't feel undeserved. Even though he was usually shy to other people's touch, he let her grab his chin.

'Let's forget about Simon and talk about your lips. I've been wanting to play with them for such a long time. You need to keep them moist if you want people to notice that lovely Cupid's bow of yours. It's all in the lips – you know how they always say tits and teeth, but I believe you can do it all with your lips. Especially when they are nice and plump like yours. Now let's see if we can make them soft.'

Helena pushed him into one of those cubicles and told him to sit down before she closed the door behind them and started rummaging through her make-up bag. He had always been fond of those bags made of fake leather or worn velvet, the layers of different kinds of dust they were covered in, the traces of glitter they often left behind and the sweet childhood smells of the various products, all of them the result of a longing for control. For making the rules about how people saw your face. The belief that by applying these different layers of colours and creams handsome chimney sweeps would start dancing on the roof to the beat of your own imagination. Not unlike Mary Poppins and her carpetbag, the contents of a make-up bag could do anything.

'Relax your lips. No pouting, there's just the two of us here. Let me soften them a bit and remove the dry bits.'

After rubbing his mouth with a wet tissue, Helena was slowly massaging his lips with a lip balm. Jimmie was glad he could surrender to her gentle movements and the occasional scratch from her purple fingernails.

'This stimulates the blood flow. You're basically getting a free erection here. You know the way girls swell when they're happy. My grandfather once told me that the poor women back home in Barcelona would rub a bit of chilli on their lips – can you imagine how painful that would be?'

She laughed and Jimmie could tell she was excited, that her body was ready for something. He wanted to ask her what her plans were for tonight, but instead he just breathed in the smell of her hair and skin. Out on the sales floor he had never realized she moisturized with cocoa products, and Jimmie was overcome with a warm sensation of bodily comfort, like an animal that had eaten without restraint.

'Now listen. Never start straight with lipstick or lip liner. That's always a mistake, because you want to use foundation first. I hope you're not ticklish.'

She started powdering his lips with a bit of her own colour.

'Our skin is almost the same, so this should work. I always think that you must have Sicilian blood to be that dark. Even your hair. That's Sicilian hair, Italians don't usually have such good hair.'

He liked the excitement of her hands in his hair and her brush on his lips, of sharing such an intimate object. Some of her skin particles were now mingling with his own.

'Do you get your Cupid's bow from your mother or your father?'

One of her fingers was now slowly moving across his upper lip and Jimmie imagined sucking it, but he didn't like those purple nails. It wasn't the right colour for an erection, and it formed a strange contrast with the orange of the toilet walls.

'Not my mother's, I don't think, and I don't know what my father looked like.'

'Look at you! Aren't we all the children of a whore? I love it. Let's put some lip liner on, make sure you go a shade darker than the lipstick. And don't be afraid of using too much – as long as you keep things moist it will be fine. And to make your Cupid's bow perfect we'll make a cross at the top, make the lines even. And sharp.'

'Are we playing priest and boy?'

'Don't talk, my dear. We don't need ash on our foreheads. Time to leave all of that behind.'

This was closer than Jimmie had ever been to such a perfect body, and it felt good to be guided by her. Helena had surely never been the last to be picked for a team during PE classes, and if the Ancient Egyptians had been right and the gods' bones were made of gold, then Helena was shining from within.

By the time she had applied a generous amount of her Romantic Cherry Blossom lipstick and was adding some finishing touches with her make-up brush, Jimmie had convinced himself that he could try to be something for her.

'Your lips are really good now, Jimmie. They're perfect.'

She leaned forward and was about to say something else when Jimmie looked down at the floor and saw that the leather of her boots was so thin that her toes were showing. Saw that she was just like the rest of them, poor, a bit pathetic and driven by the illusion that someone would discover their existence one day. Her nails were made of plastic, her hair colour the result of a deliberate chemical reaction, and her mind filled with the same old fantasy of turning a man like him. He wished he was one of those martyrs who had been roasted alive, that his constant disgrace would at least serve a purpose.

Helena's deep smile vanished abruptly when there was a knock on the door, the loose bolt shaking like a lost promise.

'The other toilet is blocked. Will you be long?'

'We're just putting on some make-up.'

'Shouldn't you use the ladies for that?'

'We are a bit of a mixed couple.'

Helena started laughing before she turned around and opened the door, her delicate body unable to shield Jimmie from Daniel's eyes. He was still wearing a yellow hoodie at that time, his curves more on show than under his smart new shirts, and from where Jimmie was sitting on the wobbly toilet seat Daniel looked beautiful, with something in his eyes that he had never seen before. Jimmie looked down again, too aware of the absurd amount of colour on his lips.

'It was meant to be a surprise,' was all Jimmie could say once Helena had stepped outside and Daniel had quietly locked the door behind them again.

'A surprise?'

'You said you liked it.'

'You realize that we are at work?'

'Do you prefer rich children's nurseries?'

Daniel moved a step closer and Jimmie now looked up, some of his dark curls sticking to his lips and the new thing in Daniel's eyes growing more intent. Jimmie blushed like a girl newly aware of her riches.

'You're very dangerous, my friend.'

Jimmie wished he had enjoyed the reality of Daniel's desire, his blood rushing, finally there for him. His hips longing to push forward. Jimmie knew that he'd wanted to feel Daniel's hands in his hair, to open the belt beneath his hoodie and to pull down his stripey underwear. To reach for his cheeks and to breathe in the unfamiliar smell of his cock. To touch his testicles, which seemed somewhat too small. And yet he wasn't quite ready when Daniel perforated his reality and entered his mouth. When he could still see the absurd shade of Romantic Cherry Blossom from the corner of his eyes, leaving stains on Daniel's cock as he gave in to a desire that seemed justified in seeking its relief.

'Could you hurry up, please? There is no loo roll in the ladies and I'm not lucky enough to get two-hour toilet breaks.'

Standing at the window and coming out of his reverie, Jimmie smiled at the memory of Elin, his favourite wankeress, interrupting.

Jimmie pulled away from Daniel's cock, which tasted like a day's work, and spat into a piece of toilet paper before he tried to clean his lips. Daniel looked down at him with the horror of a man who thought he had a reputation to lose, his eyes now fearful and his own pleasure a mistake he was longing to correct. Jimmie pitied him, and like a wounded creature he lacked resistance to this sudden contempt for his own weakness.

'I'll bring some over for you. Just go and I'll be right with you.'

In the ladies, Jimmie looked at himself in the mirror while listening to Elin's angry stream of piss. His lips were all smudged and he looked like a failed clown.

'Are you all right, Jimmie? That's a pretty wild lipstick from what I can tell. Didn't know you were a fan of The Cure.'

'I'm just exploring my beauty.'

'They'll fire you for these endless breaks one day.'

Elin left and Jimmie rubbed his lips a little longer to remove any traces. He entered the corridor that led back to the sales floor when Helena suddenly appeared in front of him. Her warm smile had returned as she handed him a chewing gum, and he couldn't help but admire that she must be close to achieving the ultimate goal: to fuck the way she masturbated.

'You might want one of these. Was this the *casting* you needed the lipstick for?'

'Why are you still here?'

'I couldn't help but listen to your mini performance – you sounded a bit like the pigs in one of my father's stables. I used to watch them as a child.'

Today Elin wasn't there to save him from his own fantasies and to remind him of his duty to give endless hand-jobs to strangers on the phone. To soften those waves of discontent without drowning. But he sensed that neither the sky they all had in common nor the two women with their excited foreign tongues would break the secret of his silent mutiny. Jimmie tried to compose himself, because he knew that nobody wanted to fuck sadness. Because sadness is the thing that stinks of unwashed clothes and oily hair. Dirty pillows.

Jimmie understood that his body had lost resistance, had softened from within, and that the cavities beneath his eyes weren't merely filled with sorrow but increasingly with disease. With infection and pain. When his knees and feet ached, it was the beginning of decay, a first sign that this absence of comfort would remain.

Jimmie took one last glance at the sky. The clouds that survived each darkness without harm. It was time to leave the kitchen with its strange afternoon silence and to wait until the later hours of the night before he could escape into his own mind again. Time to face a few more hours in the knowledge that no regret would halt the fading of a wasted day.

Sitting back down on his broken office chair, it seemed like he had travelled back through time. He almost expected Wolf to have grown a beard by now and to look like Heidi's grandfather. Or maybe like the strange goatherd who was found with animal hair in his underwear. Maybe that's why Wolf had had to leave Germany. Maybe he had violated his grandfather's best goat. Wolf and the only creature he had ever loved, a handsome lady mountain goat called Bellezza. The day they sent her lover away she had no choice but to give herself to some undiscerning buck called Hans who never learned to appreciate the extent of her beauty. In the strange overhead light, it almost looked like there were tiny horns growing on Wolf's bald forehead, his suffering pushing into the world like a creature that wanted to break free.

'Are you fond of animals, Wolf?'

'Why are you asking me that?'

'No reason. Maybe because of your name?'

'My name isn't actually Wolf. It's Wolfgang. And I don't really care about pets, but when I was younger, I had a budgie. My mother bought it for me.'

'I always feel so sorry for them. They are so much like us, trapped in a cage all their lives.'

'But they are stupid creatures. Their brain isn't even the size of a walnut.'

'Were there any mountain goats where you grew up?'

'Mountain goats? I grew up in a city, Jimmie, why would there have been goats? You should be picking up that phone instead of asking me all those questions. You know that they have changed the rules and no longer pay for hours with such poor attendance. Simon has been very strict on that.' Wolf shook his head, this time at Jimmie's apparently walnut-sized brain.

Jimmie was amazed that the Germans had found a way to think of themselves as superior not just to so-called Southern Europeans, to guest workers and their lazy ways, but even to birds and their inferior minds. He wanted to learn more about his feathered fellow sufferer, whether they had also invented specific insults for him, tailored to his home and habits. Whether he too had been called a *Katzelmacher* and a lemon-tree shaker to belittle what they didn't understand.

If only the phone would stop ringing so frantically.

'Thank you for waiting. My name is Jimmie. How can I help you today?'

'I'm in a boutique hotel in the Marais, and I'm pretty sure they're mocking me here.'

'The hotel staff?'

'Yes. They're not even trying to hide it.'

'Are you sure they're not just French? Most of them are born that way, they can't help it. Best to think of it as club foot or a rare skin condition – I always like to imagine that they're secretly unhappy about it. I'm sure they would love to be friendly and have empathy. It's your lucky day if you don't find them pleasuring themselves at their desks during working hours.'

'Is that common?'

'We had to let a member of our French team go.'

'And then they go around telling everyone about their famous love lives. Their red wine and their cigarettes.'

'I guess we all need stories to make it through the day.'

'I swear that pretty little waitress was making fun of me for going back for seconds at the breakfast buffet this morning.'

He could see her, just like he had seen himself in his mother's old summer dress that day. Other people's eyes feasting on him like wasps. He could still feel the sweat prickling his scalp as he wobbled down the street in her tiny shoes, constantly aware of his own body, of the belly he would never be able to suck in. He could hear the sweet wrappers rustling in her bag, the same wrappers he always found at the bottom of his own, stubborn witnesses of the fleeting moments of solace he always tried to forget about. He had never understood the calories the wrappers kept count of, making him feel like his belly had been filled with those stones they used to kill the Big Bad Wolf. His body was a burden and his sweet desires a sin.

'I'm sorry about that, madam. I can assure you that nobody likes French people. And I promise you that not all of them are slim.'

'I wish they'd teach in schools that overweight people have feelings too. We're not simply objects of ridicule, you know? There is a story behind our shapes.'

'But we can also be a source of joy. If you've ever watched a video of a fat person running away from an angry rat you'll know that this is our redeeming feature. We've turned our grief and our trauma into something that everyone can see, that people can laugh about. I always find comfort in the idea that the world would be quite boring without us. And you don't want to grant the French the final victory and make me call the hotel to tell off the waitress, right?'

'I guess that would be the real humiliation.'

'Think of us as witches and wizards. Alchemists. People who have found a way of turning their affliction into gold.'

Jimmie still remembered how, one day, as they had been sitting in the hearse on their way to a Bulgarian funeral, Nobes asked him whether he had been bullied at school. Jimmie was distracted, and even though he was allowed to make up his own stories, he was struggling to remember what his relationship to the Bulgarian woman in her fifties hit by the 98 bus had been. The question caught him off guard.

'You're a bit of a sensitive kind. And a fatty. Like one of them Labradors, you know – they can never stop eating. It can't have been easy at school, what with your foreign hair and your funny last name and all that.'

Jimmie always liked to think that he and Mr Nobes had made each other feel less alone. That, in spite of their differences and his concerns about many of Mr Nobes's aesthetic choices, they had created a space between them that mattered. The skin on his knuckles was flaky, his nails always a bit too long, probably with bits of dead people stuck underneath them, the warmth of those bodies now just a memory lingering on other people's fingers. Maybe it had been his same old mistake of confusing work with a place where you belong. Maybe he had behaved like a stray cat once again, confusing pity with a place to stay. Even Nobes had found a lover to share his blanket with. He sensed that Nobes would not be interested in the full story, because nobody ever was. Not even Jimmie himself. And so he mumbled something about hormones and the tragic death of a grandmother and how he had shortened his surname to something others could pronounce, and how there had been other fat children at school. He served him a manageable struggle, not something drastic with blood in the bathroom and online abuse, relaying just enough pain so that Nobes wouldn't ask any further questions until they had reached the Orthodox church, when it was time for Jimmie to look sufficiently bereft. And even though Nobes's question hadn't struck him right at the centre of his troubles, the fact that a man who had probably never owned a toothbrush could not imagine a life spent within the parameters of Jimmie's existence as anything but traumatic did leave him with a convenient amount of distress to mourn the untimely passing of Mrs Irina Nikolova. The Bulgarian mother who, after a failed love story with her sister's husband, had given him up for adoption when he was still too young to remember her face. The imaginary mother he was so ready to forgive that day, standing in a cloud of borrowed memories and incense. Even now her crime seemed smaller than that committed by his actual mother, in whose ridiculous outfit he had gone to walk the plank. The mother he would never be able to leave because his grandmother's life insurance had bought her a tiny flat in London and he didn't even get sick pay. He had no other relatives in this city whose untimely departures could free him from his predicament. Every time he saw a homeless person, he thought he'd seen his own future, and from where he sat now in this dysfunctional piece of service industry, far away from the ground but never far enough, neither life nor death felt like something he could perform with enthusiasm.

'Did your budgie have a name?'

'I'm trying to work.'

'Sorry. I'm not really feeling it today. It's not easy to talk people out of their issues all the time. Especially fat people. I don't know why we're always so self-destructive.'

'I don't think that's the kind of language you are supposed to use for people struggling with their weight.'

'We use language to protect ourselves. I haven't forgotten.'

'Good.'

'But did he then?'

'Did he what?'

'Have a name. Or did you just refer to him as the bird? *Das Vogel.*'

'It's *der Vogel.* They are usually called Hansi, but my mother preferred Bubi. And now, please, I have a tricky case to deal with.'

Probably a German who'd tripped over and needed someone to blame so they could carry on being immaculate. Much as he tried to visualize young Wolf and Bubi – had he been green or blue? Did 'Bubi' translate as an insult aimed at the bird's appearance and culture? – he kept seeing Daniel's cock and Helena's confident smile, her excited artificial lips and the little bit of real nail growing beneath the false purple. He also saw Daniel's strangely undersized testicles, which were more like little bumps than balls, an imperfection that inspired no tenderness in him. Whenever Jimmie thought about genitalia without being aroused, he could never help but think that all existential angst came from between people's legs and the fact that things were so desperately ugly down there. Some people even had the audacity to shave, as if holding a flashing sign to their flaws would make them less obvious. As if they could hide in the spaces flickering between oblivion and despair.

'How's it going, Jimmie?'

He was holding the strawberry gum between his fingers, ready to stick it under his desk to wind up the disgruntled Portuguese cleaner, when Fatiha appeared in front of him. Aware that he was holding a souvenir of his encounter with Daniel's cock and Helena's smile, he blushed and put the gum back in his mouth.

'I thought there was something in my gum.'

'Nothing I haven't dealt with before. My brother managed to get gum stuck in my hair the other day.'

Jimmie liked looking at Fatiha. If he'd had a sister, she might have looked like her. He always thought that her childhood and early youth spent in Austria had done nothing to make her resemble Wolf or any of the other Germanic people he had to deal with. As with Daniel, he found that they were all connected by the same sea, as if by looking at those Mediterranean waves they had formed a bond that could be felt across the conflicts they were meant to carry in their hearts. Raised on the same colours, Jimmie felt something he didn't have to explain, and so he was grateful for Fatiha's Moroccan roots. Unlike Wolf's unforgivable accent, he liked the slight Viennese undertones that her tongue produced when she spoke English. They never made her sound like she was about to send a pack of angry dogs after him.

'Did you end up like Lisa Simpson, with layers and layers of different solutions in your hair, until your mother finally had to shave it off?'

'You've got to stop with those references. You know we didn't grow up with the same TV shows.'

'I always forget that you are about twelve. You know, I usually object to people who were born in the nineties?'

'I was actually born in 2000.'

'Please don't make me cry.'

'Come on, Jimmie. You're not that old. And I'm sorry if I laughed about your MacGyver reference the other day. I'm sure you loved your Tamagotchi and that some of your other childhood stuff would be supercool right now. You must have had some great bumbags. And I love your lipstick, by the way.'

He leaned his chin on his hand and made his best Puss in Boots eyes. 'You're probably right. I'm only about two hundred years old. When I was in the nursery back in Italy and some of the other children teased me for being too young, I always told them that they would die before me.'

She laughed the way he had done when he was still at drama school. When he still thought that life would have mercy on him, before he understood that all he could hope to achieve was maybe to die with his own teeth.

'Were you already funny as a kid?'

'No, I think I meant it back then. I had a very basic sense

of time and bodies. I can't really picture much else of my time at the nursery any more.'

'It's hard, isn't it? Especially when you have moved countries in between. I sometimes don't know whether my memories belong to Vienna, London or Casablanca.'

'I'm so envious. Mine are all linked to my mother and her unpronounceable grief. I think she's the only country I've ever lived in.'

Before Fatiha could articulate the question that was forming between her eyebrows, Simon was already signalling for them to break up their illegal gathering. As if shooing them away for looking too foreign, for threatening his well-oiled workforce with seduction and unrest. Like good pigeons they obeyed, hopeful that they would find their own roof one day.

Jimmie returned to his screen and pretended to look at all the emails he never answered. All that failed prose, the broken poems and the sad rhythms. He couldn't understand what was meant to distinguish the so-called native speakers, those with the comfortable mother tongues, from those with the foreign tongues. Strangers that came from other shores, from overseas and beyond, that had grown up with different stories. The alien tongues that were accused of doing so much violence to their new habitats when all they did was try to be like the good ones. Yet people took them for an invasive species and not the same piece of muscle as their own. Red with those wet streaks of blue at the bottom.

Even his mother could write more legibly than most of his customers. She knew there was a difference between a verb and a noun. Maybe it was just the fear of being the alien, the other, that always made Jimmie spell things correctly. It was the fear of being discovered that made him quickly check how to spell 'lose' and 'choose' before texting back, and he always spelled out his surname instead of saying it. The good tongues didn't need to bother with that; no mistake would ever threaten their claim or their status. It was in their blood and in their documents, and they could act without shame because they had invented the rules of their own game.

He had never been able to reconcile himself to tongues, not since the day his grandmother had taken him shopping because his mother couldn't. It was his grandmother's fault that he kept his teeth shut during the few chances he got to make out with strangers. That he was afraid of the kind of invasive intimacy other tongues demanded. Because that day, she took him to the butcher's shop. He had to stand next to her and hold her hand while she leaned over and almost fell, breasts first, into the display, her heavy frame swaying as he looked up. His hands started to shake when he saw them, the bigger cows' tongues next to the smaller ones, those belonging to their children. Calf and mother finally reunited, only separated by different price tags. Even here youth was more desirable. He remembered the two neat rows and how you might enjoy poking one if it was still alive. A muscle without skin, moist and uncovered.

An instrument for the senses, delicate and vulnerable, hidden behind solid teeth. He couldn't believe how long they were and how heavy they looked. How far back they must reach into the throat, maybe all the way down to the belly, keeping the darkness down there, alert and trusting. He had felt his own tongue retreating at the thought that they were there to be eaten, like eyes and fingers and noses. His hand tried to wriggle out of his grandmother's grip as she discussed the best way to soften these pink pieces with the butcher lady. Her one fake tooth was shining too white in the midday sun, like a snow fox lost among lesser creatures. Both his hands and his forehead were leaning against the glass, staring at what he had apparently been raised on. When the butcher lady offered him a free slice of mortadella he refused, unable to take his eyes off the reality of Sunday lunches at his grandmother's house. Now he knew why he had never liked her food, why he had always found it coarse and hard to swallow: she had been feeding him another creature's ability to show affection. What she had done was even worse than what the witch had done to Ariel, and he started crying when she ordered one of each, mother and child, pressing each of them to demonstrate their freshness. Maybe they had still been alive when it happened, the tongues cut out first to keep them nice and juicy, all to keep women like his grandmother heavy and content. He couldn't stop his tears even when she told him to stop, and the butcher lady started laughing at him the way you do when you think belittling someone counts as tenderness.

He never forgot, and as his grandmother dragged him out of the shop, embarrassed because she thought him too old for tears, he felt something harden amid his sensitivities. There was something he couldn't forgive about the unexpected violence of his circumstances. Those mouths filled with blood and the darkness they no longer tried to hide from him. All that beauty he could no longer see.

'Have I ever told you how my grandmother died?'

'Jimmie! Simon will go nuts if he finds out we're calling each other. You're not even supposed to know how to do that.'

'I was just thinking of her and how she made me a vegetarian against her will. Still makes me laugh when I think of her despair. *How could you do this to me, Jimmie!*'

'You've definitely told me that story. You might even have put on the same Italian accent.' Elin always remembered everything, like an angry elephant.

'But have I told you how she died?'

'Is this another one of your European stories? You should keep it for one of your special American customers, they love that kind of stuff.'

'It was a Sunday, and we were all having lunch at her house. You know, one of those Italian gatherings with lots of aunts and too much conversation. We were outside in her garden, eating one of those sweet tarts with that kind of lemony filling when suddenly she said: "I was stung by a bee." And those were the last words she ever said. I was stung by a bee. *Punta da un'ape*. The place was too remote for an ambulance to arrive on time, and we had no idea she was allergic. She kept that hidden all her life. And so she just died. Suffocated on the day of the Lord. Killed by one of his smaller servants and without a priest there to absolve her of her sins. She's probably still in purgatory.'

'That's not a very cheerful story.'

'She wasn't a very cheerful woman. Maybe it was God's revenge that she died from the swelling of her tongue. She was also too big. It's all because of her genes that I look like this. It skipped a generation – my mother has been spared – but now look at me. It's like a curse.'

'It's also because you're a lazy bastard, Jimmie. Stop blaming your dead grandmother.'

'All right, Elin, I love you too.'

She hung up before he could, and he wished that he could spend just a day of his life with her rage – no wonder she was so slim. Jimmie was far too gentle to burn any serious calories; his fat cells knew that deep down he didn't have what it took to change. He was like one of those indistinct shapes wallowing in the ocean, living off whatever floated into his mouth, content to carry all sorts of other creatures on his back so long as they didn't tell him to move any faster or to pull in his belly because an elegant shark was approaching. Down there, it didn't matter. He imagined the dark to be quiet and forgiving, a shade of black that would turn blue in the sunlight, like in the background of all those holiday shots. Down there Jimmie would be out of the unhappy tourists' reach, blissfully unfamiliar with the distress that is caused by a sea view that is at best a partial sea view and that shouldn't have been advertised as a sea view in the first place.

Jimmie had no intention of digging out their template about sea views but, since their system did not allow them to delete any emails, he moved it into Fatiha's inbox and marked it as being in progress. He loved winding her up and he was still a little sore because of all her jokes about his MacGyver references and his youth. His childhood, with its impossible haircuts, was now far away enough to be fashionable. He had become a relic of a different age, something that wouldn't make the window of a charity shop. He had reached the point where his age would only seem young if he killed himself or died from a tragic illness. Too young to die, but also too old for everything else. Too old for a successful life and the satisfaction of a wild youth. Too old to tell anyone that he had once been a skater boy or a nymphomaniac. He didn't have the authority of an older body, proud of the signs that age transforms into dignity and that would have allowed him to jump queues and have questionable political views. He knew that he would never be a silverback but would always be lost between the ages. Unable to grow up yet old enough to know that the sensation of youth only becomes enjoyable in retrospect, when the sight of fresh and delicate bodies that seem to consume each other like infinite resources forces you to admit that your own has long crossed that line.

The phone was ringing again, and Jimmie wished he could be in a different place where people were given the luxury to follow their own thoughts without constant interruptions. He sighed before picking up the phone, wondering whether his friendly customer service personality would forever be lodged in his throat. Whether it would take a sea witch to cut it out before he would ever be able to hear his own voice again.

'Thank you for waiting. My name is Jimmie. How can I help you today?'

'You didn't answer my email.'

'I'm sorry, sir, we are very busy right now, and it takes us between forty-eight and seventy-two hours to respond to written complaints.'

'But my holiday will be almost over by then.'

'Is it something that I can maybe help with over the phone?'

'Possibly, but you will have to look at the email as well. I've included some pictures that will help illustrate the problem.'

The voice was old enough to be accompanied by one of those greying beards with yellow strands, or not really yellow, more like a faded green, remnants of a life fast becoming fragmented. Jimmie imagined the same colour toenails sticking out from worn sandals. A lonely traveller, perhaps a birdwatcher or an amateur geologist or some such tame pursuit. Possibly even someone who didn't ever pretend to be having a great time. Jimmie knew this was a rare species.

'Let me just find the email.'

'I don't usually complain, you know. And my wife would never have allowed me to make this call, but this is my first holiday since she passed away last year, and here I am. Making a complaint.'

'I'm so sorry for your loss, sir.'

Even though the old man wasn't there with him, Jimmie put on one of his better funeral faces. He liked the frailty of the voice he was hearing.

'Thinking of her now, I feel bad for sending you those pictures. I'm not some kind of voyeur, I was maybe a little overwhelmed.'

'They're downloading. Let me just... Oh dear! I see. And this is directly outside your window?'

'Yes, I can see directly into their bedroom from my balcony, and they don't even draw the curtains. I don't know where else to sit in the evenings – the room is so stuffy, and I don't much fancy going and sitting in a bar. My wife was still alive when we booked this holiday.'

'People always look so silly when they try to look pleasured, don't they?'

'I have to say that I'm not entirely convinced by their performance.'

'They probably know that you're watching, and it turns them on. Have you tried speaking to the hotel staff about it?'

'No, I'm too embarrassed to do that. Was it even legal for me to take those pictures?'

'I won't tell anyone.'

'Thank you.'

'One other thing, and please don't get me wrong. I know that you're still mourning and everything, but is there no fun in it for you?'

'I'm seventy-nine. Too old for this kind of desire. It doesn't seem right after all these years. I married my wife for a reason. I never wanted to be one of those men.'

In moments like this Jimmie always thought of himself as a saintly whore, allowing for desire in impossible situations. It was not the first time that his job had made him feel like he was giving generous relief to broken people in melancholy circumstances, but for the first time it seemed to make sense. As if there was redemption in this shy erection.

'I don't think you should be afraid of those inclinations. There's nothing wrong with them. If anyone sends me pictures of a pensioner giving himself a little hand-job on a balcony in Athens, I'll make sure they'll be deleted. I promise if you promise me to enjoy yourself.'

'I'll try, but it still doesn't seem right. If my wife knew…'

'I'm sure she did.'

Looking at the pictures, Jimmie couldn't actually make out very much; the old man's hand had already been shaking when he took them. All he could see was a man taking another man from behind, their skin too flushed and sweaty to look professional. Nothing his former French colleague would have rated, but still enough for Jimmie to indulge in the beauty of two men fucking each other in the soft light of an early summer evening.

Jimmie had known as a child, sitting next to his grandmother as she watched *The Bold and the Beautiful* or some other soap opera, that he wasn't into blondes. He admired long legs and firm breasts as he might admire a beautiful animal, but he didn't think about them when he started touching himself. And yet he could relate to the horny old man on his lonely balcony in Greece, to the feeling of others judging his desires. He had never fancied who he was supposed to – those youthful, hairless Greek boys didn't really do it for him. Deep down, he knew that he wasn't interested in perfect bodies with creamy outlines. Neither did he fancy those big leather daddies that he had first come across as objects of ridicule in nineties comedy formats before seeing them in the flesh during one of his few ventures into London's famous nightlife. And much as he liked to fantasize about slim and serious Simon spanking him in the meeting room behind the kitchen or at his desk after hours, Jimmie knew that what fascinated him most was probably the fact that Simon had managed to buy his own car and that his own mother probably approved of him. But in his heart of hearts Jimmie knew that he liked little chubby Mediterranean men, pear-shaped and with chests hairy enough to conceal a golden necklace. That made him feel like he belonged somewhere. Men like Daniel.

It wasn't clear to Jimmie why he fancied those men. It had just happened. A sudden desire not to fuck the way God had intended. He first had these crushes in the nineties on Italian beaches where men were overgrown with hair and self-esteem, wearing nothing but body oil and tiny Speedos. The golden chains on their arms and necks signalled that they were ready to be seen wearing nothing but their jewels. Ready to fuck like heroes because the gold dangling from their necks was a sign from God. They didn't have to be afraid of the Virgin Mary, Baby Jesus or the Holy Spirit watching because they had the right to get off, and with their heavy chest hair and their blessed cocks bathed in holy water they were only two doors down from heaven. In the evenings, they would wear bumbags. Functional bumbags that left their hands free to keep hold of their ugly children in public. They were good husbands and sons, and one day they would be respectable dead ancestors.

When Jimmie had first spotted the necklace around Daniel's neck, he hadn't cared that as a Jew he was probably carrying a Chai or a Star of David, that he was holy in different ways. He saw his curves, the fatherly gestures he spoke with, the chest hair beneath his slightly open shirt, and was ready to succumb.

'Have you ever had a proper job before this one?'

'Unfortunately, Wolf, I'm not straight out of drama school. I used to work at a funeral parlour.'

'Jimmie! Can't you be serious for once?'

'But I am being serious. I worked at the John Nobes funeral parlour. I can give you his number if you like.'

'And what did you do there? Play the ghost?' Like all good Germans, Wolf couldn't resist laughing at his own joke.

'I was hired as an actor to play a mourning relative or friend at poorly attended funerals. It's an extra service that Mr Nobes's family has been offering for generations. Funerals are all about dignity, you know?'

Jimmie was sure Wolf had no idea. The inquisitive German always struck him as a rather pagan creature, and back home in the mountains they probably offered their dead up to the remaining eagles or threw them in the river at the end of winter.

'Sadness has always been my speciality. I was so good that I even got to do a few Jewish services. Most funeral actors never get that far.'

'Why did you get fired?'

'I didn't get fired. I think Mr Nobes wanted me to take over the business. He had no children, and he was always worried what would happen after he died. Then he started changing my job description, and when my mother started to get involved, I decided to quit. For personal reasons.'

'To come and work here?'

'It's difficult to get acting jobs, or any kind of job really, if you look like me. The dead couldn't see me. They didn't mind.'

'If you ask me, Jimmie, you need to work on your personal reasons. Sounds like you let go of a perfectly good job with solid prospects over some drama of yours. You should be more careful next time.'

'It wasn't exactly like that. And it's not true that Italians are dramatic twenty-four seven. I would have liked to see you in my stead, being forced to wear a —'

'Is that chewing gum in your mouth?'

'Helena and Daniel gave it to me after our last meeting. I'm sure that makes it all right.'

'*Ach*, Jimmie. I know that you are kind of Italian, but rules are rules.'

Jimmie wanted to tell him that in his mind the chewing gum still had a faint aroma of Daniel's cock, but instead he pretended to roll it up in a piece of paper and when Wolf returned to his screen he leaned forward and stuck it on the handle of his colleague's chair. He had the satisfaction of knowing that one day this would wind up the cleaner.

'At least we killed our own dictator.'

'Excuse me?'

Hung up by his feet. The one dictator who had gone topless, and they hung him up by his feet. The brutal act that allowed the Italians their nostalgia for the dark years. It often seemed that this violent death had not served as closure but instead reminded people of their Duce's human side. How he deserved some compassion because it was never acceptable to turn a face into pulp by unleashing an angry mob onto it. In death, even the vilest heart has the ability to move us, to remind us of our own shortcomings. Jimmie's grandmother – as she stood in the kitchen holding her electric knife, her fake tooth shining as she cut the cooked remains of unrecognizable creatures into edible pieces – had always told him over the noise of the machine that Mussolini hadn't been that bad. The politicians they had today were worse, and at least Mussolini had cared about Italy's well-being rather than his own.

He wondered whether Wolf had also had a grandmother with a fake tooth and an electric knife who told him not to speak ill of their dictator. But then the Austrian dwarf had remained a monster right up to the end, with his suicide, the poisoned dogs and his unfucked wife. Right up to the day when his delirious chauffeur and assistant set him alight in a Berlin courtyard, some of his ashes mingling with rubble and the first days of summer. Maybe this had been the crucial difference between their two leaders. Just as the dog that went after your flesh becomes a pet again the moment you kill it with your own hands, a killed dictator is not without endearment. Something that time inevitably wraps in sweet layers of forgiveness and pride.

Jimmie couldn't help but wonder what kind of pain Simon would inflict on him during their chat later. Would he tie him to a chair or lock him up overnight, like Wolf's former colleague? He knew that this kind of scenario had become unlikely, even in a place like this. Nowadays things were more delicate. In modern companies like Vanilla Travel Ltd, pain arrived in more acceptable costumes; there was no need for shiny bruises and missing parts, no need to touch him to cause damage. In this new world nothing was tangible, and when Jimmie couldn't breathe he only had his lack of self-care to blame. When his inner supports broke there was nothing to stop him from going under, nothing but an absence of success and stamina that had left his ideal self in ruins. He didn't know how to make those inner cracks visible, but he was sure that the hierarchy would leave him exposed. He wasn't a respectable man like Daniel. Nobody had ever seen Jimmie in a shirt. He was the one who had worn lipstick. He'd overstepped the rules that held this office together and defined it as a place of restraint. There was no point in asking Helena for help, to talk to her about what had happened last Friday; she would sacrifice him like one of her father's pigs because she knew that Jimmie was not in charge of this story, that his truth was fickle and ready to bend in her direction. It didn't matter that while they were in the orange cubicle he had wanted it less than Daniel. Only the brave get to impose their own stories. But today he would face Simon and be proud of his transgressions – he would tell him a story – like a rat coming out from beneath the floorboards suddenly aware of the power its vile little body holds.

'Thank you for waiting. My name is Jimmie. How can I help you today?'

'This is a bit of an unofficial complaint, but I'm sure other women have had the same issue.'

'Could you confirm where you are?'

'I'm in Agadir. Beautiful resort really. Except for the men.'

'Is there a problem?'

'Not so much the men in the souk, but the pool boys. I have to say I'm rather disappointed. It's not really acceptable for a hotel of this rating.'

'I'm sorry about that. We operate a zero tolerance for sexual misconduct policy with all of our partners and I will escalate this to my supervisor right away.'

'Sexual misconduct? I wish! These pool boys are worse than nuns. I've not been harassed by a single one of them.'

'You're calling because you haven't been harassed?'

'That's not the word I would usually use, but I'm travelling on my own and it's never been this difficult in the past.'

Raised by women, Jimmie had been pro-vagina for as long as he could think. Even if they did nothing for him erotically, he had always acknowledged their struggle and taken Elin very seriously when she explained her monthly blood or complained time and again that female masturbation was still a taboo. He thought of 'wankeress' as an honourable title. But this time he sided with the pool boys and their refusal to serve their customers between their ageing legs. All those lonely and entitled bodies with unfulfilled dreams, flashing their power like shiny weapons. It was enough that he had to endure these people on the phone and that in his weaker moments they reminded him of his own struggle.

'Would you excuse me for a second while I speak to a colleague who is an expert in all things Moroccan?'

He was longing for a voice not yet driven by the urges of a fading body.

'Jimmie, did you move that ridiculous email about the sea view into my inbox?'

'Listen – I have a lady on the other line complaining because the pool boys in Agadir are refusing to offer extra service.'

'And now you want me to give you an opinion on the pros and cons of female sex tourism in Morocco? On the exploitation of the Other as a continuation of colonial practices?'

'Something like that.'

'Tell her that her arse must be really ugly if not even the pool boys want to fuck her. They even tried it on with one of my friend's Austrian aunts last summer. Your lady must look worse than a Mozartkugel.'

'That's only half helpful.'

'Do you want me to call my cousin and ask if he can do the job?'

'Really?'

'Of course not, Jimmie! Tell her that magic happens when you try orgasmic breathing. Just breath and muscle engagement, no pool boys needed.'

'I think that calls for a special training session with Simon. And let me know if you ever have a cousin going spare – I'm rather keen on pool boys.'

'I'm hanging up now.'

He already missed Fatiha's voice.

'Sorry, madam, it took me a while to get through to our expert on subtropical sex tourism, but I hope you enjoyed the music. She suggested that the world has changed and that you should try a special breathing technique instead. It's better to self-soothe than take advantage of others. She said that a bit of focus and muscle engagement can be life-changing.'

Before Wolf could badger him with any more questions about his failed career as a funeral director, Jimmie signalled to Simon and was granted permission to go on a toilet break. Five minutes alone with his body, his smells and his sensations. Five minutes to let go of everything. All these people who loved avocados and moral outrage as much as cocaine yet were unable to be grateful for what life had offered them. The reluctance to be content or appreciate their wealth. Soon he would be alone in this big, ugly building with only the Portuguese cleaner and the downstairs security guard sitting beneath his shiny sunset poster to protect him from the busy silence.

Jimmie was scared of being alone on the top floor of this fake office building, and he always hesitated before accepting the late shift. Before admitting that he had no life. He wasn't so much trying to keep his job – by sacrificing those precious nocturnal hours traditionally dedicated to large amounts of fun – as trying to get as far away from his mother's waking hours as he could. To live in the same house but on different planets. He wanted to make sure she was asleep when he came home, to avoid her body and the questions it produced. He often thought of her in moments like this, when he let his cock hover over the toilet bowl, his belly blocking most of the view. He almost always thought of her when he looked at his own body, which was so different from hers. She didn't take after his grandmother. Her skin was soft, her forms filled with harmony. She had cheekbones and he had never known her to have more than one chin.

It was the smell of her urine in the morning that had always made his stomach turn. It often smelled worse than any of Henry's many regrettable offences. It was like a competition, as if they were fighting over the territory of his affection. Even if he had always known that Henry was a slut on paws, purring with disdain, Jimmie had found it easier to love him in spite of his shortcomings. He had accepted this rejection by a beautiful creature as natural, and cleaned up after him without asking for emotional support. But his mother, who was equally beautiful in human terms, had never inspired that kind of devotion. There had never been anything holy about her, and any chance of worship had died between the sheets of her eternal grief. Every attempt to be close to her, to find her inside the maze she had built around herself, had made him feel even more rejected than Henry's snooty refusal to warm his feet at night. He wasn't yet able to imagine a parent's inability to love, to think of happiness as an emotion that your body refused. He'd been unable to understand that something could stand between you and the world, that you could lose your own child in those mysterious corners of your own mind.

As he grew older and understood that loneliness begins to show on bodies like wrinkles, when he'd started to shop for painkillers with a childish excitement, knowing that the little pills contained even more happiness than the sweetest sweets, he began to sense the consequences of a broken heart. The traces of a body that couldn't cope on its own. That needed little miracles to make it through the day. The little miracles that she kept in all those tiny boxes in her room and that he hadn't had the heart to steal when he'd decided to take her lipstick the night before. And once he had put his trousers back on and was ready to leave the toilet cubicle to let go of this bit of intimacy in between the overflowing bin and the teenage music, he decided to reapply his mother's red – not sharp and fuckable the way Helena liked it, but unrefined and sudden. More like warpaint that glossed over old wounds.

Looking at himself in the mirror, he thought of Daniel. *Hamud.* He didn't like what he had witnessed earlier, the difference that a step up in their grim hierarchy made. He would lose his smile next and start resembling Simon, a theatrical expression painted over a layer of wax. Jimmie missed the way Daniel used to look, like he was mourning a close relative. Like Daniel's good Jewish god had told him not to be vain and he had obeyed him with a million imperfections instead of sporting ironed shirts and a sharp four-millimetre head shave. Jimmie touched his lips in front of the dirty mirror, and it felt like the gentle sensation he had been longing for since last Friday, ever since he had received messages telling him never to mention what had happened. He was being asked to accept it as the unfortunate ending of a series of mistakes. *Hamud.* To deny that his body had inspired desire, had created a response in another's. To deny that, for a moment, Daniel's skin had been the warmest creature in the room.

Jimmie had touched Daniel for the first time that afternoon at the rich people's house in some ridiculous London neighbourhood. They were in the birthday child's bedroom. It was too warm, and Daniel had asked him to help with his red and white make-up because he could never find the right balance between horror and fun. His dignity could just about handle the oversized shoes and how well his round shape suited the occasion of being ridiculed, but he could not face the prospect of being an offensive clown. Jimmie reached for the sponge and make-up sticks as if he was about to treat an injury.

'Are Jews naturally funny? Like Italians?'

'We don't have much reason to be jolly. I'm sure you know that.'

'At least people take you seriously. When you say that you're Italian people just laugh – it's like you were born with a red nose.'

'Only your nose didn't get you turned into ash.'

'Is that why you guys are so opposed to cremations?'

'We don't own our bodies, Jimmie. They belong to God. That's why we don't interfere with them. No tattoos and no cremations. Our rules are older than fascism.'

He liked that Daniel couldn't move while everything inside him was now moving at a new speed. Daniel's body was communicating with Jimmie's like two animals independent of their owners, independent of their minds. Two manatees engaged in a silent dance, their bodies leading the way through the darkness of their broken eyes.

Jimmie moved his fingers up towards Daniel's golden necklace and looked at it.

'Will your God be very angry if I interfere with your body for a bit?'

He couldn't kiss Daniel's lips because of all the red and white on his face, and he was still nervous about other tongues and how they compared to those in the butcher shop. So Jimmie bent forward, grabbed Daniel's hand and started kissing the inside of it. Gently sucking on his palm, he let his tongue play games with Daniel's most delicate lines.

'Don't. Please. I'm not that way inclined.'

'Doesn't it feel like a distance you could walk? Or are you just worried how your hard-on will make you look in front of the kids?'

Wolf wasn't at his desk when Jimmie returned from his toilet break, so he took the liberty of drawing a wobbly little cock on one of the blank pages in the middle of Wolf's neatly arranged notepad. Much as he still enjoyed blackening the teeth of famous people on posters that had not yet been replaced with a screen – small acts of vandalism that made him believe those public spaces were his too – there was nothing like the joy of using a sharp German pencil to draw a cock on important people's paperwork, to remind them that their shoes were oversized too.

'My name is Jimmie. Thank you for waiting. How can I help you today?'

'I had no idea this wasn't a cottage.'

'I'm sorry?'

'I don't care about surfing.'

'I gather you're in one of our surfers' lodges in Cornwall.'

'I just wanted to be by the sea.'

'Do you want me to send you a list of local activities?'

'I came here to write, but have you ever heard of a serious work of art to have emerged from a surfers' lodge?'

'I'm not an expert.'

'The sea is one of my main sources of inspiration. This vast infinity, ready to crush you at any point. It's intrinsic to my work.'

'I hear there's plenty of that in Cornwall.'

Jimmie pictured a man in an old black suit with deliberately unkempt hair too long to exist within any corporate structure. He could see a scarf as well, probably red, embellished with one or two moth holes. This artist had never reached his peak, like a blossom that had started to rot before it could reveal its beauty, suffocated by the shadows of more successful plants.

'On top of that, the place is filthy. There's sand everywhere. I'll never be able to finish my draft in such a mess. I'm wary of what I'll find in the drawers.'

Jimmie always wondered about the desire to conquer these temporary spaces, to unpack your bags and pretend you'd never left home.

'I guess a bit of sand is part of the appeal of a surfers' lodge.'

'You don't understand. I'm running out of time if I ever want to get published.'

'I'll make a note to ring the cottage management tomorrow morning and arrange for a cleaner to come round and pay special attention to the drawers.'

'What about tonight? I can't work like this.'

'I'm afraid that we can only call emergency services in case of rodent or cockroach infestations. Sand doesn't really qualify.'

'Are you sure you want a negative review from a professional writer?'

'Are you really going to put on some Mozart, light a candle and turn your skills as an artist into a negative review about sand in a surfers' lodge? Published exclusively on the website of a famous booking agent, written in the great tradition of Woolf, Dickens, Shakespeare and Nigel, fifty-three, from Kent?'

'How dare you! I'm sure this novel will win a prize one day! I want to speak to your manager.'

'I'm afraid he is currently spanking someone else.'

'Excuse me?'

'I'm sorry, I meant that he is speaking with someone else and that we are about to close for calls from the UK, so please call back tomorrow morning to resolve this issue. I'm so sorry we couldn't find a solution for you today, but I would be honoured to feature in your masterpiece *The Beach and the Sand* and I promise you that I will look out for it. But for now I have to go. Thank you for your call. Enjoy your holiday and goodbye.'

Jimmie had spotted Wolf talking to Simon, and he could tell with every fibre of his oversized body that they were talking about him. It was a feeling that had never left him since school: the feeling of being more visible than others because his body took up more space. He knew how big his clothes looked on the laundry line and he could always sense the look on people's faces when they watched him eat, trying to understand what had made him so fat. Those looks inspired guilt even when he was eating by himself, just like the innumerable diet books written by slim people and the simple mathematical formulations they thought could make him beautiful in their eyes. Jimmie could never forget that his organs were covered in bad fat, that his curves were bleeding the NHS dry. He was letting society down by inviting damaged knees, heart failure and diabetes into his life like friends at a mad tea party. Unlike others, he couldn't hide his vices. And he was sure that Wolf, true to his origins, was acting the part of the innocent little cog in the wheels of a mighty dictatorship. And this dictatorship was as miserable as all other dictatorships, hollow on the inside and mostly made up of sad male bodies. Nothing but cruelties and uniforms with the added taunt that their uniforms were ill-fitting hoodies – no fancy Hugo Boss stuff for them – and it wasn't possible to be made Gauleiter here. Wolf didn't understand that they weren't rivals, because any notion of hierarchy was simply another tool in Simon's box. They were all equal in their uselessness, and Daniel was the first person ever to get promoted from regular agent to supervisor. It broke Jimmie's heart that Wolf was trying to stand on his shoulders, thinking that there was a way for him to lift his head above the water. That he was trying to show off an impossible trick, like an overly eager seal in one of those entertainment parks with tortured marine animals. Jimmie knew that neither of them would ever be one of the sexy instructors in a funky shirt but always a creature with their dignity lost along the way. Sick of their confinement but also too dependent on the bucket of rotten fish to stage a revolt.

'I'm off, my little gigolo. See you on Sunday?'

'Can I ask you something, Helena?'

'Depends.'

'Is it true that you've identified the mystery caller?'

'Not quite, darling.'

'So it's just a myth?'

'You shouldn't ask so many questions.'

'Then why do you have this kind of freedom?'

'People talk too much in this place. It makes them ugly.'

She slowly ran a finger down his cheek until she reached his chin, her other nails slowly following suit.

'Do you know how to suck a dick like Marilyn Monroe or James Dean?'

'Is that another thing you want to teach me?'

'It's the easiest way to survive in this place.'

'So you just met with Simon in the ladies to negotiate your freedom?'

'I thought you'd know me better than that by now.'

Helena's grip grew tighter before she pulled her fingers away, her nails leaving little dents in his skin. Jimmie kept looking at her, and for a split second she allowed her muscles to play with something like sadness before she stood tall again and smiled under those perfect lines in her face. 'I'd always use the men's. Less traffic in there.'

Before Jimmie had a chance to ask more questions or assess the value of his own oral performance, Wolf came back to his desk and Helena raised her eyebrows, ran her fingers across his cheek again and walked off to find the next person's fantasies to wrap around her glorious shapes.

'I think Simon wants to talk to you.'

'I know. We arranged for a catch-up during my break.'

'Be careful. He seems a little irritated. There is a rumour that someone exposed their private parts in the men's toilet. Do you think that's true?'

'I don't understand why anyone would want to do that. And it's called cock, by the way. Not even my mother speaks of "private parts" any more.'

'Looks like Simon is not the only one who's in a bad mood. Must be the end of a long week. But don't worry, my shift is about to end.'

He could tell that Wolf felt hurt in between those headphones that always looked too big for his bald head, like the oversized ears of a creature that meant no harm. But before Jimmie could say anything Wolf had accepted another call, and it was simply impossible to judge the emotional state of someone who spoke German – everything he said sounded like an entire nation which had forgotten how to dream.

'Jimmie, I'm afraid I need you to come with me now. I forgot that I'll have to leave early today.'

Simon was leaning again on the little wall that separated Jimmie from Wolf's desk, his knuckles shining red and his nails neatly cut. It was easy to imagine the contempt he had for those who chewed on their own flesh.

'Let me just mute my phone and I'll be right with you.'

Jimmie followed Simon's long, ascetic legs and he could tell from his gait that he was tense, like someone about to kill vermin. It was an unpleasant but necessary task, and the only thing that might stop him was not compassion but fear of staining a good shirt. Simon might as well have carried an axe and a black bag with which to blindfold his victim. Jimmie knew that he wasn't about to be offered a hand-job and a hot cocoa; this wasn't going to be a bit of kinky fun. He was here to get fucked, and not in a good way.

But somehow that didn't matter too much, because Jimmie felt like his body wasn't enough to hold all the sensations. As he walked behind Simon down that pathetic corridor, with his colleagues' voices now struggling at a distance, pushing against the thin walls like waves without a storm, this mass of flesh and fat and water didn't seem like the sum of all he had ever seen and touched and feared. Why did it matter what he'd done last Friday, or two weeks ago, or three days after he was born? He'd been a different person then, with a different heart and a new mind awakening with every sun. And tomorrow he would no longer be the person sitting at the conference table they used to make people like him feel small. By tomorrow, he might finally have talked himself out of this job, trying to save his lover, while people like Simon would carry on sitting there until the rising waters swallowed those edges of land they had destroyed with their own ambitions. Jimmie would no longer be there, because this world was just one version of many.

'Thank you for taking the time for this, Jimmie. It's much appreciated. And please feel free to eat, since this is your official break.'

'Can we try to get through this without any kind of formal language?'

Looking at him up close, Jimmie realized that behind those 1950s glasses and the stern eyebrows, Simon was probably younger than him. A boy trying to act the adult, one of capitalism's eager little helpers.

'Fair enough. Daniel is in a training call anyway, and there would have to be two of us here to make this official. Just think of this as a chat, and remember I have always supported you. Even when we realized that you seem more Italian than you are.'

'Would you say the same thing to someone who's Scottish? My dialect is as good as any other – the Italian language that you're thinking of is an artificial construct. A technique of violence.'

'Yes, but most of our Italian customers don't understand a word of what you're saying.'

'I don't see how I'm responsible for that.'

'I'm sure you know why we're here, Jimmie.'

'I don't know why everybody keeps talking about it. And I didn't think Wolf would care. He seemed pretty hostile towards his childhood budgie.'

'He was actually trying to help. We are all concerned about you, Jimmie, but we have to take this seriously.'

'It's all my mother's fault. She's the reason I'm sitting here today, and she was also the one to raise me in this strange dialect, so maybe you should be talking to her.'

'Are you trying to say that she made the complaint?'

'I thought we were talking about my cat.'

'Your cat?'

'Henry. My mother always hated him – he wasn't the cleanest cat. Always shat in the corner next to the telly. But still, I think she overreacted.'

'I remember Daniel mentioning that you had a cat. What happened?'

'She got rid of him. It's still difficult for me to talk about it – he was my only emotional support.'

'I'm sure he will be happy with his new owner. His bad behaviour could have been a sign of distress.'

'New owner? There is no new owner. Little Henry is with the angels now.' Jimmie lifted his eyes to the ceiling, but only briefly. Just a gentle touch, because Simon didn't look like a man depraved enough to appreciate Catholic gestures.

'You mean your mother killed your cat?'

'She lost her temper.'

'Is that even legal? And why not just take the poor fellow to a shelter?'

'We don't have pet shelters in Italy. Most cats get drowned in buckets when they're still kittens – life is rough there. And poor Henry had offended her honour with his constant violations. There was no other way. We're hot-blooded people.'

'They always struck me as responsible pet owners when I was there.'

'Cycling in Tuscany doesn't count as going to Italy. Naples, for example, used to be famous for its boiled cat skulls.'

'Surely they don't eat cats there any more?'

Nothing like a Brit worried about their concept of barbarism. What about the puppies they fed with dead animals in their nutritionally complete food? And all the brutality beneath their finery? Every dictator had a beloved pet and every queen a dog she would mourn more than her closest relative, and so they burdened countless beasts that they had captured and caged with their empty hearts. Jimmie could tell that the ginger boy too possessed a willingness to sacrifice his siblings in exchange for a better chair and a slightly more polished spoon. Their empathy reserved for those creatures they thought would never leave, that seemed to love them even when they were met with cruelty. Even when their so-called love kept leaving the same traces. The same fears and the same amount of blood and vomit on the kitchen floor.

'When people are poor, they eat anything. Birds, cats, monkeys. You have no idea what life is like in some parts of Italy. My grandmother was eight when she had to leave school to go to work, and, even so, she couldn't afford new teeth when she lost hers. We had to buy her one of those electric knives so she could cut up her food.'

'Look, Jimmie, I understand that things are a little difficult for you at the moment, but you should have come and talked to either me or Stuart. And now that Daniel has been promoted, you can speak to him as well. We are both being trained in HR management.'

'Did Daniel not mention anything?'

'Not that I can recall.'

'We talked the other day, I believe it was last Friday. I must have sensed that he was becoming more important. He was still wearing a hoodie though, which, if you ask me, suits him much better than those new shirts. I mentioned Henry to him. Now that I think about it, his blood was almost the same colour as my lipstick. You know how a cat's blood is always a lighter shade than you expect?

'My cats never died that way.'

'It's not very sensitive of him not to pass it on, to make me go through it once again. I know you all think otherwise, but I'm trying really hard to make this work and to satisfy the needs of our customers. How would you feel if your own mother had beaten your pet to a pulp in a fit of rage? When I was younger, I heard the neighbour's children torture a kitten and I couldn't sleep for days. Even though my grandmother kept telling me that they were mindless creatures with tiny brains and that I was too old to care, it still gave me a fever. They swung him around by his tail as if he was a toy and the more pain he was in, the more they laughed. That's the thing about cruelty – you're blind to it in your own house, and it's always other people who were born with brutal souls. That's what I thought until I heard my little Henry on our kitchen floor. He didn't meow, as you might think. The last sound a cat makes is actually a growl, deep and fierce because they fight right up to the end, even when blood is already shining on their noses. The look they give you, Simon! There's nothing like the eyes of an animal you failed to protect. They only have their instincts to get them through a situation, and they die with so much sincerity because they don't know what death is. They have no god or some other philosophical nonsense to reconcile them to their fate, and there's no relief until their blood stills. He just kept looking at me. My little Henry, thinking he'd been betrayed by the one human he offered so much comfort to, just because my showers always take too long and I thought it was safe to leave him in her care. I ignored the signs, her strange behaviour over her first coffee. When I came back, he was there, looking straight at me, his blood all over the floor. Humans are not as brave as my little cat, exposed on those kitchen tiles, unable to display his usual elegance. I held his white paw for hours after he died, I could feel it getting cold and stiff. Everything about him was a reproach. I let him down, Simon, I let my little Henry down.'

Jimmie let his tears run across his lips, let them mingle with his snot like a slow funeral procession. They met with his mother's lipstick and formed a first, contagious drop on the sterile boardroom table. But this time Jimmie wouldn't get off so easily. Compassion, unlike anger, liked to climax on more than a dead cat, and this was not the time to stop. The performance was not over.

'But then my mother is the victim of her circumstances. Our circumstances. It wasn't her fault that we were forced into exile. If only we hadn't bought that electric knife for my grandmother.'

'Do you want to talk about it?'

He could tell Simon was trying to find a tissue, but the room was not equipped for bodily fluids and Jimmie tried to compose himself by taking a breath.

'I've never really spoken to anyone about it. I've always felt so ashamed.'

'This is a safe space, Jimmie.'

As Jimmie was staring straight into Simon's blue eyes, he felt like he was depositing something there. Like one of those beetles that leave their eggs underneath people's skin, he would fill Simon's delicate iris with images, little seeds planted over time that would end up forming one of those dark outer rings. A sign of sorrow, as his mother liked to call them.

'It was an accident. That's what they always told me. I was young when it happened, and it's taken me a long time to understand what I saw. I can't ask my mother because all she ever says is that it took her beauty away. That Antonio Bevilacqua wasn't a bad man. Don't make a judgement based on what you have in front of you – she's still much better-looking than I will ever be. The only dress of hers that I can fit into is from around the time I was born, and even that's tight. My father, Antonio, was one of those possessive little Italian men with chest hair and a golden necklace. Flamboyant in the way that I always imagine Neapolitan pimps to be – colourful shirts and a bit of a quiff, and filled with that sexual energy our generation doesn't have any more. But anyway, Antonio was a man of influence, *un uomo di rispetto*, you know.' And here he looked over his shoulder before he whispered, 'Mafia.'

Simon responded with an understanding frown.

'My grandmother had been opposed to their relationship from the beginning. "Too dangerous," she said. "We are simple people," she said. "We don't marry criminals," she said. But no one listened to her and my mother married him anyway, in a secret ceremony witnessed only by members of Antonio's family. They were married by a priest who later had his tongue cut out for cooperating with the police. That's what they do to traitors down there. *Pentito.* That's why until today I haven't been able to do tongues. They always remind me of that priest and his gaping hole. But that morning my mother was singing. My grandmother told me that my mother used to do this a lot when I was little, but this is the only time I can remember her singing in the bathroom, and I think she was trying to communicate happiness. One of those rare moments when she peeked out of her maze and even I could tell how beautiful she was when she smiled. I was always so proud of her when she managed to smile in public. That would be unimaginable today – now she is always dressed in black, lamenting whatever comes her way. But that day, she sang. And sometimes I think that's why my grandmother did it. Because she couldn't bear her happiness. Poverty does that to people. They become vengeful and deranged.'

Simon nodded again and Jimmie could smell a first hint of sweat, not the good kind of sweat that comes with pleasure or the possibility of euphoria, but the sweat produced by your nerves. The smell of physical discomfort.

'It was some celebration. One of those things where lots of relatives bring too much food, and my grandmother brought her electric knife. Everybody knew that she always had to sit next to a socket, and people got used to the noise too. I always found it soothing, Nonna muttering over her missing teeth and that vibrating blade. Now I think that it was like her sex toy, but of course toys were for freaks and weirdos back then and I'm not even sure she knew what a vibrator was. But the knife had a similar function, it was her cock in the absence of a cock – my grandfather had died so long ago that nobody really remembered him. Italian men never last very long. And so she liked holding the knife in her hand even when we were not eating. That day she was holding it too.'

Jimmie averted his face, relying on the power of invisible grief.

'But why did she do it? There must have been a reason. Or did she suffer from mental health issues?'

Simon was now fully invested in the story of poor, toothless foreigners and their kitchen equipment.

'Antonio always fingered the food before it was ready. My grandmother believed in God. Not in the way that men like Antonio do – to admire the gold and the glitter. To perv on the Virgin Mary's tits and to find justification for their actions. The men who go to confession and then carry on as usual. My grandmother wasn't like that. She took it seriously. Or at least she had seen people saying grace on some of her American TV shows and she liked the ritual. Hands in prayer, one elbow resting on her knife. But Antonio didn't care for old ladies and their needs, and, unrestrained as he was, he reached right into one of my grandmother's famous meat dishes. He went straight for one of her best bits. Sauce dripping everywhere, the fresh tablecloth soiled. And he didn't even try to lick his fingers. That's what she said afterwards.'

'But did you have to witness the actual —'

'The knife vibrating in his throat and him spitting out my grandmother's best bits? No. She had sent me to fetch something from the kitchen. I remember my mother screaming and blood mingling with the meat sauce. It made the actual meat look so real – the fresh blood spattered on top. I became a vegetarian that day. Seeing any kind of meat always brings back the sounds of my tormented father. His fingers still moving, stained with blood and food.'

'And what happened to your grandmother?'

'She died in prison. I think she died from a broken heart because her knife was confiscated as evidence, but my mother thinks that *they* did it. You know. Revenge. Vendetta and all that. To be killed by an old woman – I don't think even my grandchildren would be safe to set foot in that country. Shame is passed down the generations like madness and ugly feet, and in their eyes we are all my grandmother's children. Toothless maniacs with electric knives.'

'You're safe now, Jimmie. Such things don't happen in this country.'

'I know. You've found more sophisticated ways to kill the poor.'

Jimmie suddenly realized his food was still in Elin's rucksack. He didn't know the time, and wasn't sure whether she'd left already. He knew she would take the food with her and tell him that he was fat enough as it was. He took a deep breath and in this moment of silence he could smell his own sweat too. For the first time since he had arrived at work that day, he realized how tired he was. His body felt as heavy as it was, and he didn't care any more whether Simon believed his story or whether he would get fired for being complicit in a sexual act he still wasn't sure he had enjoyed. He was even sorry for Elin – Simon was nothing to fantasize about. The ginger boy would never understand the true meaning of devotion and he had probably never spanked anyone in his life. It was far more likely that Elin would end up pegging him instead. Looking at the way Simon fingered the buttons of his shirt now, his knuckles pale, Jimmie could tell that he was one of those men with complicated orgasms and visions of an all-encompassing mother figure. Simon was the last thing he needed right now. And Elin didn't need him either.

'I haven't eaten anything yet and my food is in Elin's rucksack. Would you mind if I go and check if she's still there? I don't want to spend my night drinking the disgusting soup from the vending machine.'

'I'm sure she's still there.'

'Really?'

'But you go and check on your food, Jimmie. I will discuss this issue with Daniel and I'm sure we can find a solution.'

'Please thank him for being so gentle last Friday. And thank you again for listening.'

'Any time, Jimmie. But please bear in mind that this is work and that this applies to all parts of this building. We really need to keep things professional around here.'

'Of course. I hope things with Elin go well again tonight. I hear those Swedish ladies are even more exciting than their saunas.'

With these words, he got up and left, walking like a cat – the one thing he had learned from Henry, who had otherwise not always been a model feline, was that there were moments in life when all you could do was look better than your circumstances.

Jimmie suddenly remembered the clouds he'd seen from his window seat on the plane when he first arrived with his mother. The feeling that there was a new world beneath him, the colour of innocence and the texture of something soft yet strong enough to keep you from falling. And unlike the sea, which constantly tried to mingle with the horizon, to pretend that they were one in an endless struggle over the colour blue, things were clear up here. Jimmie had wished he could set foot on this promising land, and he had never got over the surprise he'd felt when the plane started going down and touched this perfect white landscape. When this garden of lightness made the plane shake and his body shiver. Hostile to the touch of strangers, the clouds made the inside of the plane go sombre, as if the passengers were being punished by angry gods for being mortals that overreached, before spitting them out into the grey reality beneath.

Wary of the toilet, Jimmie returned to his desk. Wolf had left for the day, and Jimmie felt a little pinch of remorse for having drawn a cock in his notebook – it was hard to tell how someone without a sense of humour would respond to such a gross act of vandalism. He could see that Elin was on a call and so he tried to think about the TV programmes he would stream during the late shift while listening out for emergencies and the odd call from the US, yet the image of his grandmother's electric knife kept coming back. It had been a while since he had told a story, since he'd sat in the hearse with Mr Nobes, trying out the character he would act that day. He liked to think that Nobes had been fond of his stories and not just his mother, but it's possible he might have only understood half of what he was saying because of all the complicated names and Jimmie's foreign hair. Nobes was busy longing for the imaginary days when only English people died in this city. Jimmie had been fond of him and those mornings, riding around with a dead body in the back of the car. It had felt like his stories could become real.

'Thank you for waiting. My name is Jimmie. How can I help you today?'

'I called earlier today about the Romantic Spa Break in Bath.'

'Of course, I remember.'

The dildo-cape lady! Jimmie had almost forgotten about her flying off into a liberated sky, and he felt bad that he had done nothing to support her struggle. He wasn't even good enough to act the part of Robin in support of this great liberator of the unfucked.

'Did you have any luck with the hotel?'

'Unfortunately not. Romance to them is a two-person affair. They couldn't appreciate the benefits of offering a romantic weekend of self-love.'

'I was actually just looking for some quiet time away from it all, to recuperate.'

'Do you not believe that the wounds of people who are in love heal more quickly?'

'I bet most people on the Romantic Spa Break are as much in love with their partner as I am with my toilet seat.'

'I guess it's not easy to fall in love.'

'You think I'd better stay at home on my own then and get a budgie?'

'In my experience not even budgies are faithful. They will desert you for an open window in an instant. I believe their brains might be too small to form real attachments. You can't win with them.'

He could feel her anger from earlier coming back, just as he could feel all the other people's frustration at a system that refused to accommodate their every desire. That was designed to leave them stranded before they could hit the sweet spot. It was like a recurring nightmare hiding somewhere in his brain, surfacing to ruin the mood whenever he tried to relax, like some unpopular relative crawling out from underneath your wedding cake. Jimmie found himself confronted with the eternal circular dance of production and discontent, the socks that didn't match, the plants that wilted before they improved your air quality, the dick that you couldn't suck yourself. The revolution the people on the other end of the line weren't able to envision because all they ever saw was a more comfortable version of themselves. A justification for their existence and a vague sense of achievement in an otherwise silent universe.

'You're not painting a very jolly picture there, and I don't feel like you've done anything to try to help. Don't you care at all about your job?'

'I'm sorry we haven't been able to find the perfect solution for you today, madam. I think there are lots of other journeys that you could go on that would bring you more happiness than this one. Bath is a miserable shithole anyway, full of fake museums and Jane Austen mugs. What do you want with people who took centuries to discover their own Roman baths? How about if you try ringing one of our competitors and ask if they can fly you to the moon? With handsome astronauts who caress your feet and whisper sweet nothings in your ears before you're fucked by magic crocodiles with multiple sexual organs? Why don't you ask them to make a cushion from a cloud and fan your arse with fairy wings? Or even better, why don't you all just leave me alone with your stupid fucking queries and sort out your own miserable lives?'

He took a deep breath and removed his headphones. She had hung up when he'd started to talk about astronauts and magic crocodiles and now her voice had disappeared forever in the vortex of the rotating caller system like a lost object. He mourned her, like all the precious objects he had lost on the Tube that reminded him that he'd never had the courage even to throw away a stuffed toy. Jimmie sometimes thought of how his lost objects might be thinking of him, how they might miss their warm and comfortable home. He hoped that someone might have picked them up, might have seen beyond their status as abandoned and potentially soiled. That his scarves were now wrapped around other necks and his books held by other hands. Maybe they were loved and, instead of slowly being consumed on a distant platform, chewed away at by rats and angry microparticles, they had found themselves a better home. Perhaps there had been some agency in their decision to jump out of his bag, like those cats that walk out one day, too proud to look back. Just as Henry had left him that day, most likely tempted by a slutty neighbour and feeling deserted by his mother and her new happiness. After all those years, Henry had missed her laments and her black layers, and Jimmie understood. He missed them too. He preferred her sadness to the new life she'd found outside their little family. And he could still hear the cat flap's last slap, the humiliating signal that not even a cat would stay with him. Sometimes he wished his mother had actually clubbed the bastard to death on the kitchen floor so that he could feel sorry for the cat instead of himself.

'What the hell did you do to Simon?'

Elin's rage had destroyed her last chance of looking truly lustful that day. Her lips formed an almost imperceptible line, bringing her face close to some medieval representation of death. Proof that the true colour of anger was white, not red.

'He was in perfect condition when I left him. Completely untouched.'

'He cancelled our date.'

'Maybe his mother told him not to go out with a foreigner?'

'Jimmie!'

'We didn't talk about you. It was more like a catch-up, and I told him a little bit about my family. Quite pleasant really.'

'Since when are stories about your family pleasant?'

'I meant more the conversation as such. It was fairly intimate. That's the word I was looking for.' At those words, he started pulling at his bottom lip, the one bit of his flesh he was proud of.

'Intimate?'

'We definitely shared a moment.'

'Do you really think you can seduce someone by telling them how your grandmother choked on a bee?'

'I added a few details to make it more romantic.'

'Did you mention the cat?'

'Henry made an appearance, yes.'

'And did you mention that you got ditched by your own cat?'

'It was my mother's fault.'

'You didn't look after your cat and your mother isn't well. You have to stop blaming her for your mess.'

'Don't be fooled. I used to think that too. All those years spent in dirty nighties and misery, it was all a charade. Turns out we're a family of actors. She was even wearing lipstick the day she turned up and started interfering with my life. It all went downhill from there.'

'Lipstick?'

'She was only supposed to bring me my lunch – I'd forgotten it. We'd had two funerals in a row that day but neither of them was serving proper food. You know, the kind of people who splash money on a fairy-tale carriage, pretending Cinderella has taken their loved ones for a ride, then make you starve afterwards.'

'Why didn't you just buy lunch somewhere? And what's that got to do with anything?'

'How was I supposed to know that she looked that good in daylight? And the lipstick, it's that shade of red they make from crushed beetles. Natural pigments always win.'

'The lipstick that you're wearing right now?'

'Better that way. It's caused enough damage.'

'Don't you think it's a bit pathetic to be jealous of your mother's looks?'

'Not when they interfere with your life like that. It's not about the fact that I've always looked like someone's aunt, while she had those cheekbones and never put on any weight. Those looks made me lose my job. Made me shit on my own doorstep and forced me to work in this fucking place when I could have been running my own funeral parlour by now. Comforting people with real problems, soothing them with my made-up stories. You know I would have been good at that.'

'What did she do that was so scandalous? Suck off a corpse?'

'That's rude even by your standards. You can't run a forest nursery like that. What will the parents say if you corrupt their precious offspring with such filth?'

'Look at the Virgin Mary talking.'

He formed a halo with his hands and pitched his voice a bit higher. 'I only wanted to look after dead people. They don't mind – they're docile creatures.'

'Maybe it's time to let go of those dreams, Jimmie. Maybe we don't have what it takes to make it in this city.'

'That's still not a reason to go on a second date with a guy like Simon. You don't want to end up like Helena and fuck the mystery caller.'

'And what exactly *were* you trying to achieve in the toilet last Friday?'

'It was a moment of passion. Daniel was still wearing a hoodie.'

'You know that he isn't available, right? He's married to a woman.'

'Look at us with our cheap lipstick, trying to fuck our way out of our predicaments.'

'Maybe you are your mother's son after all.'

'At least we have each other's back. I guess you accidentally rescued me in the toilet last Friday.'

'So now you want to be my knight in shining armour?'

'I should let you know that I can't afford a horse.'

'Nobody can. At least Simon has a car.'

She flung her rucksack over her shoulder and was almost at the door when another thought came to his mind.

'Elin, dear. The only real revolution is to be happy in spite of your circumstances.'

'I wouldn't fuck you either, darling.'

The last he saw of her was a middle finger, a rare letter in the language of her affection, and then she was gone. And with her the dream of being someone in another person's eyes. By now even the mysterious Danish man, whose claim to fame was that he had once worked as Leonardo DiCaprio's arse double and who could usually be found reading *The Count of Monte Cristo*, had left, and the silence was still too fresh to be trusted. Jimmie could still hear the echoes of people's footsteps and voices in the office. The red buttons were flashing mercilessly in front of his inner eye, a devil's dance that reminded him that in this place he would never be the sole master of his thoughts and feelings. He let his head spin a little more until he felt ready to fly with the devils and enjoy their infernal mechanisms. His soul being rendered useless by his daily pursuits didn't seem like a high price to pay for a bit of lightness. A lost moment of freedom that had nowhere else to go.

He was humming to himself when he noticed someone standing in front of him. Anticipating the disgruntled Portuguese cleaner, he only opened his left eye.

'I almost forgot to give you this – I was already on the platform when I realized.'

'How kind of you to come back.'

Jimmie felt immediately comforted by Fatiha's presence, and the dancing red demons disappeared into a distant corner of his mind.

'What is it?'

'I don't know. Wolf gave it to me. He said it was important to get this to you today.'

'It's probably one of his arse wipes.'

'He isn't all that bad, Jimmie. He's just German – they can't help it.'

'If you say so.'

Jimmie put the little folded piece of paper next to his mouse, wondering if it contained Wolf's long-anticipated farewell letter. *Forgive me, my dear friend, but my undying love for my sheep Bellezza is forcing me to return to the mountains. Her previous marriage to another shepherd means that we will have to live in sin, but I'm prepared to make that sacrifice. Take care, my friend. Always remember to keep your pencils sharp and your bottom clean. Yours truly, Wolf.*

'Do you fancy staying here for a bit and watching something?'

'I'd love to find out more about MacGyver, but I actually have to dash.'

'Have fun on your wild night then.'

Silence settled once more, and Jimmie decided to go for a wander around the empty office. To touch the mouse on Simon's desk and enjoy sharing the same surface with an old fantasy. Since the cleaner was taking liberties with his timekeeping again, Jimmie thought it was safe to go to the bathroom now and take more than five minutes – one of the perks of the unsupervised late shift – to enjoy some of the comfort these spaces were supposed to offer, without the fear of disturbing others with his sounds and smells. Jimmie shuddered at the thought of what the cleaner might find when he emptied those overflowing bins, but he also drew comfort from the fact someone else's job was worse than his.

'Jesus! What are you still doing here?'

'Sorry, but I spilled tea over my shirt, and I can't go out like this.'

Daniel was standing topless by the sink, rubbing his shirt. For a moment Jimmie was worried that his mind was still dancing with the devils.

'Don't pull that face, Jimmie. You know that I care about my appearance.'

'Since when?'

'Since always. There's nothing wrong with an ironed shirt.'

'Do you also change your sheets every night in case some of your secret thoughts cling to the fabric?'

'Why are you standing so far away? I can hardly hear you.'

'I'd rather not come too close, in case you're overcome by temptation again.'

Like a member of a sleeping whale family, Jimmie stood still.

'You're clearly not forceful enough, my dear team leader.

If you carry on scrubbing anaemically like that, you'll be standing there until Judgement Day.'

'Then why don't you give me a hand?'

'I'm trying to not express desire for your naked skin.'

'Jimmie, please. We've been there before, and you know where I stand on the matter. It was very hot that day, and somehow things felt different when we were wearing costumes.'

'Because it's okay to fuck a clown?'

'It can never happen again, do you understand?'

'Is this the bit where you tell me about how much you love your wife and value our friendship?'

'But I do love her. And my family is quite conservative. I can't afford any scandals.'

'I used to have a family too.'

'I know. But I can't waste my life like that. I have to take things seriously.'

'Of course you do.'

'And you got what you wanted, didn't you?'

Despite the insult, Jimmie couldn't help feeling proud that he had come up with a story to save the man who'd probably never wanted to be his lover. His balding, glittery-grey head, his golden necklace, seeming almost matte, and his curves, ready to shake with hurt and indignation, still moved him. Still made his own heart feel like an empty womb going into labour, fuelled by a desire for creation and permanence yet spitting out nothing but broken cells. A state of chaos in his chest.

'Let's not talk about it any more. Good luck with the shirt. I'll just use the ladies.'

'Wait. Jimmie. I've been meaning to ask, how did your chat with Simon go? Wolf seemed really concerned.'

'Concerned?'

'Yes, he tried to convince Simon not to fire you.'

'Are you sure he wasn't just talking about his gut flora?'

'Yes, the silent Danish guy overheard their conversation.'

'Has your call centre Mossad also informed you that Helena listened in on us last week?'

Daniel's eyes widened with fear. 'Is that true?'

'We basically had a threesome.'

'This is not funny, Jimmie.'

'I'm sure your new position of power will protect you.'

'Please tell me this isn't true.'

'Congratulations again on the new role.'

Jimmie's left hand was already touching the door, leaving Daniel to try his luck with the fickle hand dryer, when he decided to turn around. Detective Columbo in love, but without a coat. A Little Mermaid not willing to go mute and die for her lover's happiness.

'When I think about you, I do it with my actual body. It's real. I know you wouldn't stop dancing for a year if I died, but that doesn't make it meaningless.'

Daniel's free hand had frozen over the big silver button of the hand dryer, and his eyes were now as wet as his shirt. Jimmie could see the other hand shaking beneath the stained white, and he could feel his heart again.

'Forgive me, Jimmie. But I just can't do it.'

The look in Daniel's eyes made him relent, and the pity he took on him was sweeter than anything he had tasted that day. Jimmie felt like the Signora when she had finally emerged from the centre of her maze. He felt almost beautiful.

'It's okay, it's not easy to wear your lipstick in public. Go and sit over there, I'll take care of the shirt for you.'

In the absence of a functioning Italian mother, Jimmie had become an expert at laundry and broken objects, and after hitting the silver button a few times the dryer finally began to work. In the silence induced by the noise he kept picturing his mother. Maybe this was what she had felt after she left the house that day, like life was relentless in its desire to be lived. Looking at Daniel, now sitting in one of the open toilet cubicles, for the first time Jimmie admired what his mother had achieved. In spite of her broken heart. He was finally ready to accept that she simply hadn't been able to hold his hand for all of their journey together but that he could still be proud of his red lips. Daniel's chest was heavy, and he held his head between his hands. A happily married man.

'Here you go. Give me your arm – and now the other one. As good as new.'

Jimmie buttoned up his shirt with a tenderness he rarely showed himself, and when he got to the last button he gave Daniel a gentle kiss on the lips. Nothing to draw excitement. His teeth closed. His eyes open.

'Now go and be your best heterosexual self.'

'Thank you, Jimmie, dear. *Hamud.*'

'Happy to be of service.'

Daniel smiled the way some people do at funerals, with that delicious mixture of sadness and relief. It was the conclusion of an affair, and Daniel knew how to love the departed, how there was nothing like the images of those we leave behind. Images you could draw again and again until they corresponded to the corners of your own mind. And like a good corpse, Jimmie retreated into a distance that would never be conquered again.

His lipstick was now faded, like the first hours of the day. Quiet traces of a battle that would take years to leave his heart. That were deeper than the scars showing on his skin. Tiny pigments that would cut into his inner textures before they would eventually be washed away by the dark floods of time within. The circuits and desires of his most relentless muscle forcing him with every beat to try and enjoy this fucking life.

After a while, Jimmie heard his lover's vanishing steps, but he was too tired even for his own tears and the inevitable self-loathing that they would bring. He decided to enjoy his freedom and unlock his phone to check his messages and see if anyone else had let him down.

I gave your lunch to the homeless woman on my commute. She would like some meatballs with her pasta next time.

The Swedes and their fucking meatballs. He had told Elin a thousand times that pasta, especially cold pasta, with meatballs was a defilement of Italian food, and that like most defilements it came from America. Jimmie had never been, but he knew that it was a place with no culture and no real food. No real history either, apart from the violence they denied. America was an irritating younger sibling with nothing to show for itself but unacknowledged genocides and immaculate teeth. Jimmie was scared of those American teeth that glowed in the dark, and whenever he saw them on posters or in magazines he wanted to cross them out because they reminded him of the difference between a rich body and a poor one.

This was probably the right time to crawl back to the funeral parlour. Jimmie needed to come out of his sulk and share this refuge with his mother, to behave like good foxes in a den, because otherwise his poverty would bring him down. A body is only truly yours as long as you can afford to pay for your teeth and your clear skin, your flexible limbs and your clean blood. But once you start having to rely on external systems to maintain it, systems that are beyond your control and your pay cheque, your body becomes a disposable object, shared with multitudes. Jimmie was scared of these mechanisms and the body he would soon no longer be able to afford.

Staring at Elin's message, he thought of his grandmother and the bad eyes that she had refused to have fixed, the bad eyes that meant she couldn't see her own body or those of others or the direction of an electric knife. For many years before her death she wasn't able to witness her growing imperfections, the lines that age drew all over her body, the veins that exploded under her skin. The bones that seemed to grow over each other and defy her anatomy. She could have felt them if she'd wanted to, but Jimmie knew that her fingers had been taught not to trust the temptations of her own skin and that she thought of it as a sign of illness when her breath got hot. Impossible to see that bee with her eyes. She had looked so content in that fridge-coffin that sucked up several months' worth of energy, as if she had reached a silent agreement with the bee to give her that fatal sting and her relatives had all fallen for her stupid little trick. As if she had chosen to die on a sunny Sunday in June. He envied her faith in that solid body of hers and wished that soon he, too, could be exempted from having to deal with himself in the mirror. That he would simply be able to rely on others to come up with a story that would be better than anything he had ever held between his fingertips. That words would be bigger than what he had come to think of as his circumstances.

Jimmie sighed. Now he knew he didn't have any food, he was starving. The disgruntled Portuguese cleaner with the magic key to the vending machine was nowhere to be found, and, as always, Jimmie was out of change. Elin had defeated his greed this time, and he could see her with two little pink kitten bums dancing on her shoulders, laughing at his miserable defence.

Tell her to fuck off. Meatballs are for dogs.

He put his phone away. In the heavy silence of this Friday evening, he could hear his own heartbeat, like a whale that had drifted away from his family. Alone with the ebb and flow of his struggling mind, Jimmie could feel his fears growing like monsters coming out of a child's wardrobe, conquering his senses one after the other. Unable to hide behind other bodies and their noise, he began counting the hours until he could leave and the sweet melodies of his inner wilderness would recede and give in to the sensations of a world shared with others. He was almost grateful when the red button flashed and the dancing devils returned to illuminate the darkness within.

A variation.

He had a voice like candyfloss, sweet and pink. Jimmie took a deep breath. He could feel it playing with his nostrils, the warmth that immediately filled him from within. A promise of bliss that relaxed his features. There was a hand too, holding his as he waited for his candyfloss to be wrapped around the little wooden stick. A hand that had taken out a few coins and paid the woman behind the machine, a hand that made him feel small and protected. As if he still had teeth that would grow back and fingers he could lick in public. As if life really smelled of melting sugar.

'Good evening. My name is Jimmie, I think. How can I help you today?'

'This must be really late for you.'

'Don't worry, sir. I'm used to doing the late shift.'

'Just call me Alex.'

'Sure. Alex.'

'What's your name again? I always have trouble catching people's names.'

'Jimmie. My name is Jimmie.'

'That's cute. Jimmie. Is that short for something?'

'No, my mother liked it like this. It's a bit ridiculous. A name other people would give to a poodle.'

'Not at all. It's a beautiful name – your mother did well.'

'Thank you, that's very kind.'

'You must be fond of her.'

'That's not always easy.'

Jimmie liked the way he laughed, thick and warm.

'What's so difficult about her?'

'Everything. She's Italian. She's depressed. She made me lose my cat and my job. It's a pretty long and pretty unforgivable list.'

'You're Italian?'

'Kind of. We moved to London when I was young.'

'But?'

'I do have the hair, but I don't know about the rest.'

'Different days are different, I guess.'

'Yes. And sometimes I feel like I could be anything and I worry that reality is drifting away from me. Working with dead people was so much easier.'

'Did you say dead people?'

'Yes, I worked as an actor at a funeral parlour. But when the other woman called in sick – and she called in sick a lot – I also helped Mr Nobes to get the departed ready for their final outing.'

'Wasn't that quite scary?'

'You get used to it quite quickly. And trust me, it's much

scarier to deal with the complaints of people who are alive than to put a bit of make-up on a friendly corpse.'

Alex chuckled again and, judging by the sound of his voice, Jimmie imagined the greying hair that was growing on his chest. Moving up and down with only an ocean between them.

'That's the job you lost because of your mother?'

Jimmie paused to think. 'Did your parents ever make you do things you didn't want to do?'

'Plenty.'

'My mother never bothered, until recently. It took me a while to understand that we were both just trying to be happy. That maybe it wasn't entirely her fault when things got out of hand at work.'

'At the funeral place?'

'I always tried to invent a new story around each lonely corpse, but on that day Mr Nobes didn't want me to be the son of the twin separated at birth. He wanted me to be the sister.'

'He asked you to perform in drag?'

'I had to steal one of my mother's dresses.'

Jimmie had been asked to put on the biggest dress he could find in her wardrobe, the one she had worn in the final weeks before giving birth to him. True to her eternal sadness, this dress too was black. Yet he felt more protected by the dress than he ever did by her person, and for a while he just stood there, finally close to the woman he knew so little about. His belly now filled the fabric where he himself used to be, only this time he wasn't wrestling with her over that space, and he even brushed his curls to resemble hers. Emerging from that hidden world beneath her sheets, he decided to use her dark nail varnish and a splash of her perfume, breathing in the scent that made him feel like they were doing this together in a place they both belonged to.

'Mr Nobes said it was necessary to be able to offer his customers more variety and that someone like me shouldn't find it difficult. I bet it was due to my mother's new presence in his life. She always finds a way to get into people's heads.'

'Is she mean?'

'She's like one of those animals that you think are slow, but in reality they're superfast. Like a tortoise, or a wild boar. Just prettier.'

Alex was laughing. 'Sorry. Carry on. I had a glass of wine for lunch, and it's made me giggly.'

'At least you had lunch.'

'You didn't?'

'My Swedish co-worker gave my lunch to a homeless person in an attempt to make me less —'

'Chubby?'

'Fat, to be honest. I know you can't see me, but what's the point in hiding it?'

'I'm old enough to flirt with my eyes closed.'

Jimmie liked this stranger.

'Anyway. Tell me more about your mysterious tortoise-wild-boar mother.'

He had gone to work early that day. He had never possessed his mother's ability to sleep through his predicaments.

His sadness never functioned as a lullaby, nor did the stories that grew inside him like wild ivy. He often wondered what happened between those sheets when her eyes were open.

'Nobes had given me keys to the parlour not long before, and sometimes it helped me to sit with the dead for a little while. It made my performances more convincing, the stories I told about them felt more real. Like we had actually known each other.'

'I'm dying to know what story you would have told about me.'

'I've never flown across an ocean for a funeral.'

'These days, I don't live in the States any more. I'm only here for business.'

'But you don't strike me as a lonely immigrant. You don't sound stranded in a place you've forgotten how to leave.'

'Those corpses taught you a lot, didn't they?'

'More than the living.'

'Who was it that day you tried on your mother's dress?'

'An Italian man. Antonio. Rather handsome. He could have been a Neapolitan pimp.'

'Handsome like a daddy?'

'I'm not sure. I've never met my own father, but when I sat there with him' – remembering the dead man's body, Jimmie blushed – 'I did think that my father might have looked like him. The moustache, and those hands that had become rough from working in a kitchen or a field.'

'Did it turn you on?'

'He was dead.'

'That's not an answer to my question, Jimmie.'

'It's against the law.'

'To fancy a daddy?'

'To fuck a corpse.'

'It's also pretty difficult, I imagine. Things might get a little stiff.'

'That depends on how long they've been dead for. People here aren't very quick to bury their loved ones – in London you even have to queue for your own grave. Unless it's a Jewish or a Muslim thing, they're usually soft by the time we put on their make-up.'

'I love Jewish funerals. Almost more than their weddings.'

'I've never been to a Jewish wedding.'

'You should go. It's so much fun. There's nothing like a Jew on a dance floor. Don't you have any Jewish friends?'

'I do.'

'But?'

'He's already married.'

'I'm sorry.'

'It's all right. I guess I'm not really marriage material. Not so good at satisfying the expectations of aunts.'

'I don't think anyone is. Or maybe it's because I've never tried – it's always been uncles for me.'

'Thank you.'

'For what?'

'You're being too kind. You have no idea what my usual phone calls are like.'

'I'm not a very regular guy.'

'And I didn't even ask you what your emergency was.'

'That's because we were busy discussing your emergencies. You seem to have many of them.'

'I'm Italian. Emergencies are a way of life for us. But what is yours?'

Alex sighed. And Jimmie imagined his fingers playing nervously with the pencil he had found on his bedside table. The candyfloss was now a shade darker, heavier, as if it had been forced into the world on a rainy day.

'It's an ongoing emergency, if you like. It's just been too long.'

'Since what?'

'You were right earlier – I do have friends and all of that. I go for drinks and dinners and shows, but I don't have anyone to be less alone with. And now it's become a silly habit whenever I travel, and maybe it's the reason I travel so much.'

'To call emergency lines? Maybe that's what my mother has been doing all those years...'

'But I'm not good at making up stories. I haven't been trained by the dead.'

'Why don't you try a dating app instead?'

'It's always so obvious what you're looking for and can't find. And I've never gotten over the fear of all the things that can go wrong.'

'Of getting hurt?'

'I went to too many funerals in the eighties and nineties – our bodies had to witness so much sadness. It doesn't feel right that I'm still here while they're all gone. So, when things get physical, I run a mile.'

Jimmie thought of the virus they had all been taught about at school, which had somehow made its way from other animals into people's bloodstreams. He thought about how the virus had become a curse, allowing all sorts of people to say that Other bodies were ill bodies. That they didn't just bring shame but also disease. How it had marked those bodies as different, as ugly, as something you can't even expect a nurse to touch. He thought about how little had been done to protect the people that had come before him, and the frantic condom campaigns that had illustrated his own youth. The fear they'd tried to instil and the sadness he now felt when he thought about those posters, as if there was a connection that the virus and its offspring formed between people and across time. Not only this notorious virus that often travelled via people's pleasure, but all the diseases that had moved from body to body across centuries to form communities independent of family, borders or religion. That there was something that held them together, something that tore down the lines that had been drawn between all those beating hearts. These things weren't born of themselves. Nothing ever was. Whether rich or poor, all bodies were born without loneliness.

'Is that all you're scared of?'

'Isn't that enough?'

'We all have to die of something, even if you won't fuck anyone ever again.'

'You're terrible, Jimmie. You've spent too much time with the dead.'

'Haven't we both?'

They fell silent.

'Maybe we don't like being seen.'

'Are you fat too?'

'It's not that.'

'I thought so. You sound quite attractive, like you keep in shape.'

'I feel like you're reading my palm.'

'I'll be gentle.'

'What else can you hear in my voice?'

'Something that means you don't feel comfortable in your trousers.'

'Definitely getting warmer. Go on.'

Jimmie could hear him shift position: little movements to welcome each other. He enjoyed the feeling of his own erection brushing against the fabric of his underwear, the heat spreading between his legs, letting his breath carry them over the first silence.

'Now tell me what you see, Jimmie.'

'I can see your hands. Your delicate fingers. I can feel them playing with my lips, full and soft. They feel like sucking your fingers. I want you to smear my lipstick across my lips and I want to suck your fingers, Alex. I want to suck them until you're wet. I want to —'

'Be good, Jimmie. Do me like a girl.'

'Just lie down, Alex. Lie down on your back for me and

let me kiss your neck and smell your soft skin. Let me taste it, bite it. Suck it. Let me lick your nipples and feel them getting hard. Feel your skin with my skin. Kiss your whole body, your curves. I want you, Alex, I want to taste your belly and your hip bones. I want to open your legs and play with what you've got there. Can I open your legs, Alex?'

'Yes, Jimmie. Yes.'

'Can you feel my head between your legs? My hair touching your skin?'

'Yes.'

'Can you feel my tongue licking you soft?'

'Yes. Keep going.'

'My tongue is warm and wet and my hand is reaching for your sweet spot. Can you feel my other fingers entering you?'

'I'm inside you now, Alex. It feels so good to be inside you. And I want to start sucking you, Alex. Can I start sucking you?'

'Yes. Oh, yes.'

'I will leave my fingers inside you, so you feel full. Like you're exploding. And I'm sucking you now, Alex. Massaging the little bridge between your holes with my other hand so you can feel me everywhere. My fingers are moving faster inside you, in and out, and now I'm sucking you, your lips are full and swollen now. I taste you and then I go deeper. I take you all in. I'm holding your cheeks now, Alex, and you grab my hair and push me deeper. You put your legs around me and I suck you hard. My spit dripping down your cunt.'

'Almost there.'

'I want you to come for me, Alex. I want to taste your cum. Just come for me, come in my mouth. I want to swallow you. Be a good girl, Alex. Let me have your cum.'

Jimmie closed his eyes, and he could hear that their movements and sounds were in sync. He was touching his own lips and sucking his fingers before he could feel his own weakness coming on. The deep contraction that came before the moment he found impossible to remember, like the seconds before he fell asleep. Briefly changing from one state to another while still in the same body – motionless yet looking at a different set of stars. Suddenly a free luminary.

'Are you all right?'

'What's your eye colour, Jimmie?'

'Brown. But not the very exciting kind of very dark that's almost black. More like a pale brown. Like the kind of deadly, runny soil that accompanies natural disasters. You can't really see yourself in my eyes. What's yours?'

'My eyes change with the light, but I think they're mostly grey.'

Jimmie could imagine them. The kind of grey you find in the sky just after the sun has disappeared. The last bits of cloud before the real dark sets in, before the night takes over.

'I'm sure they're beautiful. Just like your voice.'

'Do you always work this shift, Jimmie?'

'Most days, yes. I try to get away from my mother as much as possible.'

'Your mother. We never finished the story of your mother.'

'I'm not sure anyone could.'

'But you were telling me a story. I'm sorry, but I've not been this excited in a long time and now I'm getting a little drowsy.'

'You should get some rest.'

'Can I call you again?'

'Just ask for Jimmie.'

'And you promise you will tell me the story of your mother next time?'

'I promise.'

'Thank you, Jimmie.'

'Sleep well, Alex.'

'You've been wonderful.'

The story of his mother. A story like many others, something that would amuse a stranger but no longer pierce his own heart. Maybe he should be happy for her, just like he was happy for Alex and for all the other old people in search of their orgasms who managed to find some relief. It was his fault too. If he had learned to take better care of his lunches, he wouldn't have had to ask her to bring it in for him the day she ended up meeting Mr Nobes, a few weeks before his life turned upside down. And she wouldn't have had to leave the dark cave of her bedroom like some creature that had forgotten to stop hibernating. And she and Mr Nobes wouldn't have seen something in each other that he couldn't see in either of them. Two sets of skin that longed for solace.

Not long after that, he'd gone in early one morning, feeling like the world was soft and open, like it could bend at the edges of what we call reality. It was his first Italian funeral at Mr Nobes's. Antonio. Their men never lasted long, as if all the good life they had been born with was eventually overcome by the kind of sorrow that blocked their veins and lungs. Until their own cells turned against all that pleasure and attacked their vital organs like an army of defecting soldiers, driven crazy with hunger and fear. Ripping apart what no regret would be able to fix. Jimmie had felt nervous that day, smoothing down the fabric of his big dress in anticipation. It was during those weeks that Mr Nobes had started arriving late, when he'd become irregular with the habits that used to define him. Jimmie was alone with a dead man who had once been called Antonio and was now lying in one of Mr Nobes's mid-range coffins – real wood but fake silk. Somewhere between a life worth living and a disgrace. An act of migration gone wrong. And looking at the still bristles of his moustache, Jimmie forgot how to act. Antonio's face hadn't even been touched yet by that most beautiful aspect of age when it doesn't matter any more whether you had once been called a man or a woman, a boy or a girl. Antonio was still of an age when everyone could tell that he had a cock, that he could be a son, a father or a lover. And Jimmie felt for him. An Italian immigrant who had probably worked as a chef or a waiter and never learned how to pronounce the words 'juice' and 'earthquake', Antonio had probably never even thought of the limits and confines Jimmie now sensed. He couldn't let Antonio go like this. Far away from home, the man needed a last moment of transgression, something to reconcile him to the untimely fading of his beating heart. To the absence of a family. His mother had always told Jimmie that dead people had dignity, that it was a sin to mess around with their peace. But Jimmie also knew that dignity was a curse, a constraint, and he came to think of his deed as an act of care. He felt like one of Jesus' famous whores, tending to a body that had been promised the gates of heaven. He could still smell the embalming cream that had been rubbed so generously into Antonio's skin, and if he was honest he could also still taste it. Jimmie preferred not to allow all his senses to remember that day, even though he had grown fond of Antonio afterwards, of the smile that seemed to have deepened on the dead man's face. He knew that he had probably committed a crime when he bent over to get closer to Antonio, that he was a fallen creature with little hope of redemption, and yet, as he felt for the peacefulness of the other's skin, without risk or fear of being judged, without the notion that a family was a performance, when he reached for Antonio's manliness and pushed his colourful shirt aside, when he kissed his skin with the delicate hair and leaned his head on his empty chest, the blood in his ears pulsing like he could almost hear another heart, he understood for the first time the intimacy of skin that was silent, that no longer held on to the mysteries of a grown body. That he could encounter without fear, confident that skin doesn't have to cover your flesh before you can call it your own. It was what love could have been.

Afterwards, Jimmie plucked a hair from Antonio's quiff and put it in his wallet behind the picture of his mother. Whenever he looked at the two of them, stuck together in this secret union, Jimmie was overcome by a sense of family.

He could still feel the fear of discovery with which he had been leaning over that coffin with his first dead Italian man in it as he tried to make everything look neat again. His hands were too shaky to fasten the last button when he sensed Nobes standing behind him. He could still feel the vulnerability of the female attire clothing his body, could still hear his mother's name whispered in that impossible English accent that shaped every vowel like their tongues were about to die.

'It's probably about time you knew that I just love smelling Maria's perfume first thing in the morning.'

If she had stayed in her bedroom that day a few weeks earlier, if she hadn't brought him his lunch, if it hadn't been for his obsession with cold pasta, Jimmie wouldn't have screamed and knocked Mr Nobes over with his heavy frame before the short-sighted man could realize that there were some unfastened buttons inside the coffin. If his mother had stayed at home that day, he wouldn't have had to run down the street in shoes that didn't fit, with the feeling that he had lost a home once again. And maybe he wouldn't have had to take himself into orange toilet cubicles to look for intimacy because he couldn't stop thinking about the sensation of shit running down his freshly shaven legs.

Jimmie suddenly realized that he wasn't alone any more, and he rolled forward a little on his chair so he could wipe away the remnants of his excitement.

'What's your name again?'

'Sorry?'

'Your name. I always forget your name.'

The disgruntled Portuguese cleaner was holding the hoover like a kendo stick again, and Jimmie was glad that he had at least remembered to zip up his trousers. The cleaner had never asked him for his name, but that didn't matter.

'Jimmie. My name is Jimmie.'

'Now look, Jimmie. I had an emergency today. My wife, she is sick. You haven't seen me coming in late, okay?'

Jimmie was about to protest and ask for a hot chocolate in return, but he remained silent when he realized that he had left an impressive stain on Wolf's keyboard.

'Sure. I was dealing with an emergency anyway.'

'Why does that make you so happy?'

'Happy?'

'You're smiling. What's there to smile about in this shithole?'

'Nothing. Sorry. I'm just tired, I've lost control over my features.'

Jimmie knew that he risked being clubbed to death with a dysfunctional hoover, but his happiness was too stubborn.

'I haven't eaten all day. I'm feeling a little faint.'

'I don't think that will do you any harm.'

The cleaner left, dragging the hated hoover behind him en route to the vending machine, and Jimmie kept on smiling, fond even of the disgruntled cleaner and his thinly disguised threats. He probably had the word HATE tattooed on his cock, but tonight Jimmie found him endearing and felt a softness for the dreams he must have once had before arriving on this island. It was the kind of sympathy you feel for people before saying goodbye. Jimmie knew that he wouldn't have to return, that Alex had set him free, because not even his best story would get him out of being immediately suspended for turning their precious customer care line into a phone box with fake tits and imaginary vaginas. He knew that emergency calls were very popular for training purposes and that having a wonderfuck at work was certainly not in the handbook. He thought that he'd done well, but he knew he would once again have to return to the bottom of the sea and wait for the waves to let through the occasional ray of sunshine. Until another disaster brought people to their knees and prevented them from leaving their traces all over the globe. No more foreign footsteps in the rainforest and no more remnants of foreign pills and euphoria in the water that runs through all cities, pets, plants and hearts.

Jimmie would wait. He would think of Alex, the stranger with the grey eyes who had made him the lover he would never be, a fantasy that had briefly walked the earth and for a moment allowed him to believe that bodies weren't real. Who had made him drift into another galaxy and taught him that love was bigger than just one heart, that there was magic in all migrations and that freedom was a luxury.

And then Jimmie decided to get up and leave without seeing the cleaner again. He turned off his computer, removed the grubby headset and packed up his stuff ready for the night bus, that aquarium of strange creatures who don't talk but forever marvel at each other's shapes and sounds. Ready to be carried off into the night, his body still and light. To be moved without any of his own commands, almost against his will.

In the dim light of the bus, he finally opened Wolf's note. It was the cock he had drawn earlier in his notebook.

I don't know about Italians, Jimmie, but from a certain age Germans have hair on their testicles. Allow me therefore to correct your artwork.

Jimmie leaned against the window as he looked down on the poorly drawn pubic hair, tree branches brushing against the roof of the bus like strangers asking for help, and he was almost ready to admit that he would miss him.

Acknowledgements

Joachim, for dungeons, falafel and everything else a writer's heart could desire.

Olivier, for continuing to allow this to happen.

Heidi, for her courage and determination.

Chris, Gabriela, Maxence and Anna for working their magic.

Nicky, for the walk in Hyde Park.

Susie, for her faith in this adventure.

Phoebe, Josh and everyone else at The Indigo Press for their warm welcome.

Fair Miriam, for saving the day.

Jane, for the ice under my feet.

Fabio, for letting me learn from him.

Andrée, Marta, Diletta, Luca and everyone at the Teatro Franco Parenti, for performing a miracle.

Camille, for all that lies ahead.

Laurence, for coming out as a dog lady.

T, for being my wife.

Sam, for being more glitter than bitch.

Stephen, for all the joy he brings into our lives.

Peter, for looking after us.

RL, for making things bearable.

Adam, for letting me read from *Ulysses*.

Florian, for our *sitzungen*.
Rahel, for the red bed.
Michael and Valentín, for making Paris feel like home.
Richard, for being our Berlin Daddy.
Milena, for our breakfasts in dressing gowns.
Katrin, for being my call centre buddy.
Camillo, for our book club.
Marya, for sharing the dream of five days of silence.
Paul, for the tea in his studio.
Rémi, for the coffee we are going to drink one day.
Matthew, for coming back to London sometimes.
Sergey, for keeping me sane.
Myshkin, for being the best little shit.
My parents, for not disowning me.
Maurizio, for sharing his life with me.

Transforming a manuscript into the book you hold in your hands is a group project.

Katharina would like to thank everyone who helped to publish *Calls May Be Recorded for Training and Monitoring Purposes*.

THE INDIGO PRESS TEAM

Susie Nicklin
Phoebe Barker
Michelle O'Neill
Will Atkinson

JACKET DESIGN

JF Paga

ARTWORKING

Luke Bird

PUBLICITY

Sophie Portas

EDITORIAL PRODUCTION

Tetragon

COPY-EDITOR

Sarah Terry

PROOFREADER

Gesche Ipsen

The Indigo Press is an independent publisher of contemporary fiction and non-fiction, based in London. Guided by a spirit of internationalism, feminism and social justice, we publish books to make readers see the world afresh, question their behaviour and beliefs, and imagine a better future.

Browse our books and sign up to our newsletter for special offers and discounts:

theindigopress.com

Follow *The Indigo Press* on social media for the latest news, events and more:

@PressIndigoThe
@TheIndigoPress
@TheIndigoPress
The Indigo Press
@theindigopress